Black Angels MC E

MW01170973

Her Crazed Possess ion

Written By Talitha Gholston

Josie Wright is damaged at an early age when her crackhead mother's pimp took her and used her to make money. After years of sexual abuse, she is saved. When she is sent to the foster home, she meets her best friend, Harmony. When her and harmony move to a small town, her best friend meets the president of the Black Angels MC. She never knew that she would fall in love with the guy who is haunted by his own sister. When her mother brings the pimp to her doorstep, he threatens everything that she loves. When she tries to leave, Harmony isn't having it. Harmony gets stuck in the middle of this war she is fighting.

Deiondre "Crazed" Williams is the VP of the Black Angels MC. When he met Josie, he saw his sister in her eyes. That is what makes him want to protect her. After she's kidnapped by one of his brothers, he wants to chase away the fear in her eyes. Holding her every night, he falls in love with her. Keeping his distance, he believes that she is better without him. When her abuser shows up with her mother, he wants to protect her even more. When everything he loves get threatened including his best friend and President of the Club's woman and child he will have to decide if she is worth it. Can him and his club keep the women that mean everything to them safe?

<u>Dedication</u>

This book is dedicated to my lord, who walks with me every day. My husband who is my strength and my rock. I love him with every fiber of my being. My son who is eighteen, but he will always be my baby. My mothers Debra Anderson and Valerie Gholston who aways support me. RIP to all my loves one lost along the way. You will always be in my heart.

PROLOGUE: JOSIE

I was three years old the first time she sat me on the curve. "Sit there you little slut and don't move until I tell you," My mother orders. I knew to listen. The last time I didn't do what she told me to do, she beat me until I couldn't move. Someone walks up to me. He looks at me then at her.

"Why did you bring the little bitch?" He asks.

"Didn't have a choice," My mother answers, nonchalantly.

"Come on you little whore," He says. I look at him then my mother.

"What are you waiting for? You heard him," She grates. "Go," I do as I'm told.

"Every time you work out here, I want her with me. She is old enough now," My mother nods. He puts me in his car, and we leave. When we get to a house a lady comes out and gets me out of the car. She guides me into a room and places me on the bed.

"Get undressed and under the covers. I'm sorry little one. Do as your told or it will be bad for you," She says with tears in her eyes. She leaves me there by myself. I'm scared. That was the first of many times that I was on camera.

******

Six years Later...

Today is my birthday but I know it doesn't matter. We never celebrate it. My mother doesn't even love me. I just came through the door and my mother is laid out on the couch like every other day when I come home from school. At least she lets me go to school. She was the same way when I left. Her pimp will be coming for me tonight. He does every night after he lets the other boys have me. There is three of them. Sometimes he lets the guys who work for him have me. At first it was just the other boys my age. He decided he wanted me when I turned five. He records us so he can make money. I don't cry anymore. No one cares what happens to me so why should I.

Someone knocks on the door. I don't answer because if I do the beatings last longer. I'm going towards my room when people burst through the door and comes inside. It's not home to me, so I don't care. If I don't get blamed, then I'm fine. "Come with me honey. You are going to be safe now," The lady says softly.

"They will hurt me if I do," I cry.

"No one is going to hurt you anymore," The nice lady says.

"This one is alive, but barely," Another person says.

"You have to save them too," I whisper as they take me out of the roach infested house. They sit me in the police car and take me away from hell.

******

They kept asking questions and I answered them to the best of my ability. I didn't know much. After two days and two nights they sent me to a group home. I'm in my room the first day when two bigger girls came into my room and stand in front of me. "You are the whore that ran her mouth," One says.

"Hey," Someone says behind them. They both turn towards the voice. "Pick on someone that will fight you back," She is not much taller than me, but she looks fearless.

"That is enough," The lady who showed me to my room ordered. My savior didn't even look at me as she walked away. That was the only time I saw her for a couple of weeks. Those girls tried me again but that time I stood up for myself. They jumped me but I didn't go down without a fight. They don't bother me anymore because I stood up for myself. That was my first fight ever.

Today they are sending me to a counselor. They say I'm withdrawing from everyone. I say I just want people to leave me alone. I don't want to talk about what happened to me. I'm sitting beside the girl who stuck up for me the first day here. She has two scars on her neck. "Thank you for defending me the first day I got here with those two girls," I say.

"I dislike bullies," She says without looking at me.

"They make you come here too," I ask.

"Yeah. They say I'm too angry and quiet," She answers.

"Me too," I say.

"How did you end up here?" She asks.

"Was raped and put on camera by my mother's pimp," I answer.

"I was raped by my mom's boyfriend. Where is your dad?" She asked.

"Don't know. My mother was a crackhead prostitute," I answer. "Where is yours?" Tears filled her eyes.

"He died over in Afghanistan," She answers.

"Damn I'm sorry," I reply. "I'm Josephine but you can call me Josie,"

"Harmony," She says back.

"Harmony it's time. Come on back," The counselor says. She gets up. She turns and smiles at me as she walks backwards doing a funny dance behind the lady.

******

We both have been aged out of the system for a while now. Harmony and I became best friends. When we both aged out of the home, we got a house together. It's true what they say, people only adopt babies. She is the only person I trust. "Harmony," I yell as I walk through the house. I'm a stripper; she is a server. People think I'm easy, but I'm not. She is the only one that knows the truth. She is very conservative. I don't believe I will ever find a man I can trust. They are all the same.

"Yes," Harmony answers from the couch.

"Let's move," I say. "We can find jobs and leave. I need a change,"

"Okay. Where are we going?" She asks. I knew I could count on her.

"I don't know. Let's see," I answer as I began my search for our new beginning.

PROLOGUE TWO: CRAZED

I was sitting in my room doing homework when I hear her. "Please stop. It hurts," My sister cries out. I'm ten and she is eight. Our mother is a crack whore who is never home. She is today and still she is high out of her mind on the couch. "Please stop it hurts," I sit there trying to ignore her cries. I'm only ten, how can I stop a grown man. I tried telling but it didn't help. He beat me after. He has been doing it since she was five and I was seven. I can't handle her cries; I open my window and climb out. I find my best friends at the basketball court shooting hoops.

"What's up?" My best friend asks.

"He's doing it again Jerome. I can't handle her cries. I'm going to kill him one day. Even when he is gone, she's crying," I answer.

"That suck. I'm lucky my mom struggles to take care of us by herself, but she is good to me," My other friend says.

"You are lucky Damien," I reply.

"If you need my help I there. Just say the word," Jerome says.

"This is something I have to do myself. Thanks though. I know I can always count on you," I answer. We play a few games of basketball before I go home. When I get to the house he is gone. I hear Toya in the room, so I go check on her. She is in a corner naked with blood and pee on surrounding her including on her body. She doesn't even look at me. I go to the bathroom and clean up the tub. I take a bunch of water to the kitchen and warm it up on the stove. When it's fully hot, I take them to the tub. I repeat the process until the bathtub is three quarters of a way full then run the water to cool it down just a little. When I'm finished with the water I go back to her room. She is still in the same place. I pick her up in my arms and take her to the bathtub. When I lay her in the water, she starts crying harder.

"Please take me away from this world. I don't want to live anymore," She whispers.

"Don't talk like that. I'm going to stop him. After I will take you away from here," I answer.

"I can't take the pain," She says softly. As I wash her up, I know what I have to do. I finished her bath and dressed her. I sat her in a seat in her room while I changed her sheets and cleaned the floor. I didn't want her to have to smell it while she was asleep. After putting her in the clean bed, I took a shower. It was cold but it helps me think. As my sister's blood and urine went down the drain my plan was set. I got dressed and went to bed. "Please stop," I heard my sister cry out waking me up. I knew where he kept his gun. Since he was police, he kept it connect on his pants. I grabbed the biggest thing I could find. I ran into her room and swung the chair as hard as I could. It connected with his back and shattered.

"You little bastard. I'm going to kill you," He said as he got off my sister. He hit me in my eye causing me to fall to the ground. He got over top of me and kept hitting me until I almost passed out. I heard the shot then felt his weight. I looked at her while trying to push him off me. She is slightly blurry because my eye is swelled from his hits.

"I'm sorry. I love you," She said as the tears fell from her eyes. They rolled in waves down her cheeks. "Always remember you saved me," She put the gun under her chin.

"Wait. We can be okay now," I plead with her. "I need you here with me,"

She looks at me with tear and pain filled eyes. "The pain is too great. I knew you were too young to stop it. Don't blame yourself. You deserve the world. Make sure you be happy," She looks me in the eyes as she pulls the trigger.

"NOOOO…" I yell as I watch in horror as my sister's brains hit the wall behind her. She crumbles to the floor. As hard as it is, I push him off me and crawl to her. I pick her up and lay her on my lap. I held her to my chest rocking as my tears and her blood covered my body.

Sitting with her in my arms, I heard the sirens in the distance. They were coming. Someone heard the shots. Where were they when they saw the bruises or heard her cries. They rushed into her room.

"Young man is you hurt?" The person asked. I couldn't let her go or look at them. "Young man I need you to look at me," I lifted my eyes but couldn't see anything but my sister pulling the trigger. "Are you hurt anywhere?" I shook my head yes. Of course, I'm hurt, I'm holding my dead sister in my arms. I watched as my sister shot herself. How could I not be okay. Why would they ask me such a dumb question. My heart is breaking for the innocence that was so carelessly taken. I couldn't see anything but my sister through my tears. My eye felt swollen from the man hitting me. "We can't get all the blood off of you until we collect all the evidence. We have to take you to the hospital."

"Why?" I ask.

"Why what?" The officer replies with a question. He looked confused.

"You didn't help us before she did this. I couldn't save her. I tried," I said, absently. They couldn't answer me. They didn't have an answer. They all failed her. I failed her. My thoughts were all jumbled up. I closed my eyes and saw her eyes as she pulled the trigger. They took me to the hospital.

That is when my tears stopped, and the anger and guilt began.

******

Eighteen years later…

It has been eighteen years since the day my life changed forever. My best friend Beast and I started a motorcycle club. Damien left after high school to travel the world. We have a meeting today about a gun shipment. We are currently at a gas station. I follow his eye path. She is fine. I look at him with my look. "What are you thinking?" I ask.

"Nothing. Let's get this over with. I'm ready to get inside of something," My best friend answers. I stood there for a second before she comes out. She is beautiful but she has that same broken look in her eyes that Toya had before she pulled the trigger.

"Toya," I whisper. She looks at me and our eyes meet. They are beautiful like the trees in the fall. I turn and get on my bike. They pulled off before us. When we are finished at the store, we leave. We got behind the SUV and they were going our way as us. They turn off a road and we head straight. We get to the diner and sit. I can tell Beast isn't in the game. "Where is your head at?" Even though I already know. The beauty at the gas station.

"Here right now," Beast says, lying. "It's time," I look up and our contact is getting out of his SUV.

CHAPTER ONE-JOSIE

I woke up this morning and he was nowhere to be found. After I gave him my body, he stopped holding me at night. I didn't mean to tell him I loved him. He thought I was asleep when he whispered it back. He doesn't talk about it and neither do I. I'm walking through the club looking for Harmony. She is currently six months pregnant. "Josie Boo!" Harmony yelled, excitedly when I walked into the kitchen. She was being herself doing a funny dance. I shook my head as I walked to her.

"You are nutty," I said, hugging her. She looks like she is having twins. "How's my babies doing?" I leaned down and say to her belly.

"Babies? You mean baby," Harmony counters. I just nodded not believing her. But if she believes it more power to her. That is when I felt his presence. I stiffen.

"Ooh. I wish you two would stop. Everyone knows you like each other. Ouch," Harmony said as we heard a smack.

"Mind your business, woman," Beast ordered.

"Make me. She is my business," Harmony retorted as she rubbed her butt cheek. "Daddy's being mean," She said while rubbing her belly. Beast pulled her on his lap. She kissed him on the cheek as he rubbed her belly with her. Commotion happened in the party hall.

"Beast, Crazed get out here," One of the members yelled. Beast got up and Harmony followed him. I followed behind Crazed. When we got into the party hall there was a guy at the door trying to get in.

"Where is she?" The guy grated. "What did you do to my sister?"

"Who is your sister?" Beast asked.

"Ashley. She was hanging around here and now I can't find her," He answered.

"She hasn't been around here for a while," Gorilla countered.

"You all are lying scum. I know you did something to her. I will make you pay," He grated. He turned his hateful eyes on me and Harmony. "Your baby will be just like them, scum," Harmony started moving towards him with death in her eyes just like a mama bear. Beast gently wrapped his arms around her hips and pulled her to his chest. He whispered something in her ear, and it calmed her.

"You need to be very careful what you say next," Beast warned.

"Just speaking the truth," The guy spit out.

"You have said enough. Time to leave," Crow said as he escorted him out.

"He is going to be a problem. Meeting in fifteen minutes. Prospect's I need you all to clean up the place," Beast ordered. "Harmony, Baby you take Josie to our room until I'm finished. You have an appointment with Doc," She nodded, and I followed behind her. When we got to her room she sat on her bed. She patted beside her.

"Spill now," She ordered.

"You sound like Beast. I don't know what you are talking about," I replied defiantly.

"You and Crazed. It's been weird since Beast proposed to me," She countered. "Now SPILL!"

"Okay. When we danced, he said I reminded him of Toya? He wouldn't tell me who Toya is or what happened," I answered. She got a weird look in her eyes as she stared at the wall. I let it go for now. "That night we had sex," Her eyes got wide while wiggling her eyebrows like she only she can do. "It was impressive. Before I fell asleep, I told him I loved him.

He thought I was asleep, and he said it back. Before, he held me every night after I had my break down. He chased away my demons. Now I barely see him, so the demons returned. What do you know that I don't?"

"I don't know the whole story but what I do know is she was abused like us. She didn't make it and he blames himself. He really is a good guy. So, you love him?" She asked, wiggling her eyebrows again. I ignore her.

"He made me fall for him by chasing away my nightmares. He made me feel safe for the first time in my life. He's not holding me anymore and the nightmares are back. I'm losing my mind. Do you know my whole story?" I asked. She shook her head no.

"I never asked because I don't like talking about mine, but I'm here for you if you need it," She answered.

"My mom never wanted me. I was three when she sat me on the curve for the first time. She liked calling me a whore and a bitch, sometimes calling me a slut. Her pimp decided he wanted me, so he took me with him. He had other kids have sex with me until the day he decided he wanted me too. I was five when he made that decision. He recorded everything that was done to me," I said trying hard not to cry. "The day she overdosed and almost died was the day they saved me. It wasn't much of saving but I wasn't raped every night anymore. My mother survived."

"You know I love you right. I'm sorry you had to go through that. I wish I could have saved you then. I love you and you are my sister. I will demolish anyone that tries to hurt you," Harmony says.

"I know. You have always been my light in the darkness that surrounds me. Even though you went through something similar, you were always my strength. You were always happy and weird. You make me laugh even when all I want to do is cry," I said honestly.

"You're going to make me cry," Harmony said as she hugged me. "If it helps to talk about it, I will always be here."

"I respect that, but you will have your hands full with these babies," I replied.

"You believe it's more than one too?" Harmony asked.

"Yeah," I answered.

"Me too. Can you imagine two Beast Jr's?"

"You know you will love that. He really is protective over you so he will be more so over them. You will get one boy and one girl," I say.

"Maybe," She answers.

"Do you still have nightmares?" I asked.

"Not so much anymore. When I met Jerome, he stopped those. Please talk to me," She pleads.

"The boy they sent in was the same age as me. I cried and screamed. He came into the room with a whip. He hit me twenty-five times on my back. After the boy had sex with me as I laid in my own blood," I answered. I turned and lifted my shirt. She gasped.

"I'm so sorry," She whispered.

"When I was a little older, he came into my room and my mother stood in the door, she told me to shut up and take it. After he was finished, I washed the blood away. She was waiting in my bedroom. She told me she hated me while she beat me until I couldn't move," I said as I showed her the scars from the belt up my side.

"Are you okay really?" She asked as Beast came into the room.

"I will be," I answered.

"Everything is clear. You girls can come out," Beast says. Harmony gets a big smile on her face.

"I'm hungry," She says as Beast helps her out of the bed. I followed them out of the room. We go into the kitchen. As we go into the kitchen, I see Crazed is at the bar talking to the bartender. I watch him as I walk into the kitchen. Beast fixes Harmony something to eat while she does another funny dance. I just shake my head as I sat at one of the tables.

CHAPTER TWO: CRAZED

After our meeting I went to the bar while Beast went to get our girls. When she was scared this morning, I wanted to hold her but decided against it. She deserves better than me. After she told me she loved me I stopped holding her. I don't deserve her love when I let my sister die. I get my drink when I sit down. I always drink the same, so our bartender knows what to make me. I watch as Josie walks into the kitchen. "You know she won't bite you right?" Gorilla asked as him and Crow take seats beside me.

"We know how you feel about her," Crow says.

"She is beautiful but damaged," I say.

"Okay, not trying to be rude but the point is?" Crow asked.

"My sister was the same way," I answered. They gave me a look. Few know about Toya. Beast, Damien, Monster and Gunner are the only ones. "My sister had that same look in her eyes every day after our mother's boyfriend raped her. She killed him, then looked me in the eyes as she pulled the trigger. I saw it all. After it was too late the police came. I still see her pain and tears every time I close my eyes. Sometimes I see her pull the trigger. It replays in my head all the time."

"I know that had to be rough," Gorilla said. "It would kill me if something like that happened to Tammy," Tammy is Gorilla's little sister. We drink our drinks in silence. When I'm finish, I call Gunner to let him know I was coming to relieve him from duty. Gunner is following the tramp's brother that helped hurt Harmony. He is a piece of shit like his sister.

"You do realize she isn't you little sister? Josie survived," Crow asks before I leave.

Turning to look at him I say, "I know but it's hard to look in her eyes and not think of my little sister. I should have saved her before it was too late."

"You were a child too. You have to find a way to forgive yourself. If not then you may miss your blessings," Crow replied. "I'm here if you ever need a friend. You are my brother. Keep your head up bro."

"I appreciate that," I say as I get up from the bar. "I will see you guys later," I leave out of the club and head to where Gunner told me he was. When I get there, he is at a place I have never been before. "What's up brother?" I stay sitting on my bike.

"Avoiding the beauty back at the club huh?" Gunner says. I nod my head. "I think we should have two of us at a time. I have been following him and he has this meeting with this guy. He looks like a piece of shit. They are planning something I just don't know what. Look they all guns. Not little guns either."

"We will talk about it in our next meeting. Go back to the club," I said. He nodded then left. I sat there and watched as the two interacted with each other. There is something about this man I don't like. I picked up the phone and called Beast.

"What's going on brother?" He said into the phone out of breath.

"I think we should have two of us on them at a time. I have been sitting here and he is meeting with someone else. I'm over here at the diner two towns over. I sent Gunner back. We need to have a meeting. Can you send all three of the prospects to Diamond's Diner in Fair folk Tennessee? This guy needs to be watched. I have a bad feeling about him. I'm going to take a picture with my phone. We need at least two on our guy and two on the other guy until we know how dangerous he is," I take a picture with my phone. "He has some muscle with him. They are packing. I have never seen him before. They are planning something,"

"Be right back," Beast said. "Stay just like that,"

"Hurry back Daddy," Harmony said as I heard a door close.

"Brink, Tattoo, Bear, and Popeye. You three go out to Diamond's Diner in Fair folk Tennessee. Crazed will tell you what he needs when you get there," Beast yelled. I know he is yelling through the club. "They are getting on the bikes now. I'm going to make a call. We need some trackers on these assholes. I will see you when you get back,"

"Okay," I answered as we hung up the phone. I watched for a while before my brothers got there. It takes about an hour to get here. "Hey brothers," I say.

"What's the business?" Bear asked.

"You see that guy?" I asked. "The one that came to the club house,"

"That's Ashley's brother. She was one of the whores that used to be in house. She was a spy. She helped our old road captain and the old president of the Devil's MC kidnap Harmony and Josie. They were going to do terrible things to them. As you know Harmony is Beast's world. When they first got together, Mac didn't like it. When they kidnapped the women, we made sure they never hurt another woman. That's her brother. We don't know who the other guy is, but we figure that they are planning to try to take our club down. They know that they can't come to our town. We have too many eyes. I need you to watch these two dudes. Follow and see where they are staying. I have to head back for our meeting. Brink, you choose who follows who. Stay vigilant. Stay connected with us so we know there isn't any trouble," I say.

"Who hurts women and children?" Bear asked.

"A lot of people do. I have to get back. I will see you soon. I will call you Brink when I'm in the meeting," I replied. I was still on my bike so take off. I got back to the club in an hour. I head right into the building.

"Where is she?" I ask as Crow walks up to me.

"She is with Harmony," Crow answers.

"Where is Beast?" I ask.

"The place Harmony loves the most," Crow answers. "The kitchen,"

"The Kitchen," I said at the same time as Crow. I turn away from him and head into the kitchen. She is facing Harmony, so she doesn't see me come in. I wish I could be the man she needs.

"Crazed what is your real name?" Harmony asked.

"That in none of your business, woman," Beast orders.

"Excuse me handsome, I was talking to him not you," Harmony says then looks at me. "Well?"

"Deiondre," I answer.

"I love it," Harmony says. A smack is heard as my best friend's hand connects with her ass.

"You don't love anything from any man," Beasts say.

"Jerome, you are my man, my lover, my soon to be husband, the father of my child, and the most handsome man in the world to me. I love only you but he has a beautiful name so I can love it if I want. I don't love him. Stop being jealous silly man," Harmony says as she kisses him. The smile on his face is contagious. She has him wrapped around her finger. I smile.

"You ever see him before?" I asked as I show the picture on my phone. Beast and Harmony both shook their heads. Josie steps over to look. Her eyes widened but she fixed her face. She shook her head, but I could see the fear in her eyes.

"Alright beautiful time to go spend time with Josie in our room. We have a meeting," Beast orders.

"Okay," She says. She kisses him then gets up. She looks at Josie and you can tell she didn't believe her either. "You are going to tell me what is going on," Harmony and Josie walk out of the kitchen. We head into the party hall.

"Club meeting now," Beast yells as he walks towards our meeting room. He sits at the head of the table. I sat in the VP spot next to him. I pull out my phone and call brink.

"Hello," Brink answers.

"Church is about to start." I reply.

"Okay." Brink says as I put it on speaker. The rest of the brothers come into the room and take their seats.

"We have some things to discuss. First order of business, we all saw the drama yesterday with the brother. I don't regret anything that we did. He is going to be a problem though. He is working with someone else. Crazed has a photo of him. Show them," Beast says as I pull up the picture and pass my phone around the room.

"I saw him before. He was eating at the diner one day when we went in to eat. Since the women have been here you two don't go anymore. It was Flight, Crash, and me," Our road captain says.

"Okay Gorilla. He is a threat to our club. Keep our sisters safe. If they have been watching us long, then they know about them too. We need to move Tammy, Tamyry, and Bridgett here until we figure it out. We have empty rooms for them to have privacy. They have escorts. Until we find out what is going on we need to be vigilant. I have a child and a woman to protect. When we leave, we need two of us to be there. I know it's not what we want but it's best," Beast orders.

"I don't mind just sleeping here until we figure it out," Gorilla says.

"Why don't we all just sleep in our rooms?" I suggested.

"That's a good idea," Beast says as everyone shakes their head in agreement. "That is settled. Next in line we always need these two men watched. We need two on each guy. The new guy seems harmless in the picture but the fear I seen come from Josie means she knows this guy. It may be someone from her past. I don't know but her body language spoke volumes. She stays in sight. If she leaves, she is watched. Harmony is a given for protection, but she barely leaves unless it's for Josie,"

"I'm with you. See if Harmony can get it out of her. We need to know what is going on so we can protect them," I say.

"Hawk called one of his soldier friends about tracking and listening devices. We need to know what is going on. When we find their base, we will buy it and track their cars. When he calls, Hawk, Crow and Crash will ride to meet him. They will ride back with him so he can show us how to use them," Beast orders.

"I can do some research on the guy's picture. My brother-n-law and his wife are FBI agents. It's my wife's brother. The only thing we need is to get his fingerprints. A name would help too," Monster says.

"Okay. We will work on the name. After we can get him taken care of," Beast says. "That is covered. I will make up a schedule of who watches and when,"

"Sounds good," Gorilla says.

"Meeting adjourned," Beast says as he hit the grovel on the table.

"Alright Brink, stay safe." I say.

"I will brother." HE says hanging up the phone. We piled out of the room.

"NO, YOU ARE NOT!" Harmony yells from the bar.

"YOU ARE NOT MY MOTHER!" Josie yells.

"I DON'THAVE TO BE YOUR MOTHER TO PROTECT YOU!" Harmony countered. Beast went to Harmony and put his arms around her. He whispers in her ear, and she calms. It always amazes me how they calm each other.

"What is the problem? Why do you have my woman stressing?" Beast grates.

"I'm leaving. It's the only way I can protect her," Josie says.

"From what?" Beast counters.

"Him," Josie cries.

"Who is he?" Crazed asked.

"I don't know," Josie says. She shuts down, realizing she may have said to much.

"Harmony," Beast says.

"She won't tell me his name, but he is from her past," Harmony says.

"You are not leaving," Beast orders.

"You're not my man so you can't tell me what to do. Yes, I am," Josie says.

"Whatever. I can't save you if you don't want help," Harmony says and leaves her standing there with tears in her eyes.

"Really?" Beast says as he takes off after his woman.

"You have serious issues," I said and walked away from her.

CHAPTER THREE: JOSIE

I was in the kitchen with Beast and Harmony when he came in. "Crazed what is your real name?" Harmony asked.

"None of your business, woman," Beast orders. She never listens to him. I laugh.

"Excuse me handsome I was talking to him not you," Harmony says then looks back at him. Beast face is priceless. Harmony was a trip when she wasn't pregnant so now that she is pregnant, she is more of a mess. "Well?"

"Deiondre," He answers.

"I love it," My best friend says. Smack is heard as Beast hand connects with her ass. I shake my head.

"You don't love anything from any man but me," Beast grates.

"Jerome, you are my man, my lover, my soon to be husband and the most handsome man in the world to me. I only love you but he has a beautiful name so I can love it if I want. I don't love him. Stop being jealous silly man," Harmony says as she kisses him. He pulls her on his lap. The smiles on both of their faces are beautiful. I'm so happy that she is happy and protected. She deserves it. She controls him so I know she will always be protected when I leave.

"You ever seen him before?" Crazed asks. He shows his phone to Beast and Harmony. They both shake their heads no. I walk over to look at the picture. When I see who it is my heart speeds up, but I cover up my emotions. I shake my head no. How did he find me? I began to form a plan in my head. I look at Harmony and she is staring at me. She has an unreadable look on her face. She is no longer smiling.

"Alright beautiful time to go spend time with Josie in our room. We have to have a meeting," Beast orders.

"Okay," Harmony says as she gets off his lap after kissing him. She looks at me and I know that she is getting ready to make me talk. "You are going to tell me what is going on," It was an order not a question. We head towards their room.

"Club meeting now," Beast yells as we walk into their room. She closes the door behind us, locking it.

"Start talking. I know that look. Who is he?" She asks.

"I can't tell you. That will only get you hurt," I answer. "I have to protect you and the babies. I have to leave." I say as my mind begins racing. "How did he know I was here? I can't stay here," I get up and start pacing. "I can't hurt these people. They are the closest thing to family that I have. I have to protect Harmony and Deiondre,"

"Josephine, slow down, you are not making any sense. They may be the only ones that can help you. You are not leaving. You can't run when something hard comes our way. I love you and you are my family so I will not stop until you are protected. This is my family, and you are included," Harmony ordered.

"You don't know what he is capable of. He is evil," I say as tears begin to fall down my cheeks. "I have to leave." She walks over to me, puts her hand on my arms to make me stop pacing and look at her.

It looks like a light bulb goes off in her head as recognition hits her brain. "He is the one that hurt you from before we met isn't he. The one you told me about?" Harmony asks. I nod my head at her looking at the ground. My mind is racing. I hurry out of the room. I feel her on my heels. "Josephine stops and talk to me. Where are you going?"

"Far away from you and my god children. I have to protect you," I say. "Why won't you let me go?"

"Because family stick together. I can see your fear. You think you can protect yourself from him," Harmony says. I look back at her and I see a sea raging behind her beautiful eyes.

"I'm leaving," I say.

"NO, YOU'RE NOT!" Harmony yells as I see the guys coming towards us.

"YOU'RE NOT MY MOTHER!" I yell back.

"I DON'T HAVE TO BE YOUR MOTHER TO PROTECT YOU!" Harmony yells as the tears fall down her cheeks. Beast walks to her and puts his arms around her. He whispers in her ear. I know she will be safe with him, but I have to leave.

"I'm leaving. It's the only way I can protect you," I say.

"From what?" Beast asks. I can't tell him and put him in danger. Harmony loves him too much.

"Him," I plead. Hoping they could just understand.

"Who is he?" Crazed asks.

"I don't know," I answer. I can't tell him because I love him, and I don't want him hurt.

"Harmony?" Beast asks.

"She won't tell me his name, but he is from her past," Harmony answers.

"You are not leaving," Beast orders. I don't have to listen to him. I'm not his woman.

"You're not my man so you can't tell me what to do. Yes, I am," Josie says.

"Whatever. I can't help you if you don't want the help," My best friend says and leaves me standing there with the tears rolling down my cheeks.

"Really," Beast says as he takes off after her.

"You have serious issues," Crazed says and begins walking away.

"You don't understand," I cry. He stops and looks at me. "No one understands."

"Then help me understand. Who is this guy?" Crazed asked. I shake my head and rush out of the building. I get in my car to leave the impound. I sit there and let the tears fall. I close my eyes and see the ragging sea in her eyes. I get out of my car and go back inside. I go to my friend's room and knock on the door. Beast opens the door.

"Are you ready to tell us who he is?" Beast asks.

"He isn't someone good. I don't know his name. I just know what he does for money," I answer. I'm not lying. I never knew his name. I was never allowed to call him by his name.

"Seriously," Beast grates.

"Calm down baby. When you get upset, I get upset. She's telling the truth," Harmony says.

"I'm. I was a kid when I knew him. The only thing I was allowed to call him was Daddy, Master, or Sir. He was my mother's pimp and my enslaver," I answered.

"Okay. You don't have to say more if you Don't want," Beast says. "I get it now. Why don't you girls go out and get some things. I will have Rider go with you girls. Don't go anywhere else but to get a few things. I need you two safes. "I nod my head. I can tell that Harmony is still mad at me, but she doesn't say anything. Beast follows us out of the room. When we get into the bar Rider is at the bar drinking. "Rider, can you take the ladies to the strip mall. They need some air,"

"I got you," Rider answers.

"Stay safe," Beast says as we follow Rider out to my car. We get in and drive to the strip mall. Harmony and I were walking in the downtown Centre when the one person I never wanted to see again was walking towards me. I grab Harmony's arm. She looks at me.

"What's wrong?" She asks. When she looks at my eyes, she follows my line of sight. "Is that who I think it is?" I nod my head. She pulls out her phone and calls Beast. I know that because he is her man. He is very protective of her. "Hey baby, I know. Listen I need you to come down to the strip mall," She paused for a second. "Now. I will explain later," She hung up the phone as my mother approaches us.

"Hello Josie," She says.

"Donna," I say disgusted.

"Close enough," Rider says. She sneers then backs up.

"What is this? I'm Donna now," Donna says pointing at Rider.

"When you're not much of a mother that is what you are called," Harmony snapped. Donna sneered while rolling her eyes at her. "I can make those stick in the back of your head. Roll them again. I don't like you."

"You look good," Donna says turning back to me.

"No thanks to you. Why are you here?" I grate.

"I didn't have a choice. He made me. He has your sister," Donna says like I knew who that was. I don't and I don't care.

"Hello Josie. My Josephine has grown up to be beautiful. You will make me a lot of money now," The one voice I still can't get out of my head says.

"She won't make you anything asshole," Harmony barks. I grab her to protect her from him. I can't let him hurt her.

"Who is this beauty? I might keep her for my myself," He says.

"You won't be keeping anything," Rider grates as he pushes us back further. I look at my mother and she stares back. There is something in her eyes I just don't know what. She never did love me. I could see pain in her eyes, but it's not for me. I hear bikes getting closer.

"Get away from her," Harmony grates as he moves towards me. She puts me behind her. I'm glued to the spot as she gets into mama bear mode. My muscles tighten, the hair on the back of my neck, as the fear creeps up my spine. He looks her up and down.

"You are a little thing. I will take you for her. We can call it even," He says as he tries to reach for her.

"You will step away from my woman before you lose that hand," Beast grates as him and Crazed comes to stands in front of us. "Fall back Rider. Get the car."

"Beast." He snickers. "I heard a lot about you. You have to be Crazed. The one that wants what is mine. Brian told me all about you, but I already knew. I've been watching you. You will regret threatening me. You are standing between me and what is mine. Now I want her too. I have friends in places scum like you would never know and they work for me." He is a monster that haunts my dreams.

"It doesn't work like that." Beast grates. "If you know what's good for you then you will stay away from my woman."

"We have to get out of here," I whisper to Harmony. "It's him," She just looks at me. I'm guessing she already knew. She is very perceptive.

"The bastard that hurt you," She speaks a little too loud. I nod. "I should kill you." She is going towards him again. Beast grabs her.

"Go get in the car now," Beast orders moving Harmony behind him to safety.

"Go with her," Crazed orders. Usually, I would have a smart remark but not this time. Harmony pulls me to my car that Rider drove up. He takes us directly to the club house. Shaking like crazing even with being safe, Harmony touches my leg.

"You're pale. You're safe now. Calm down love," Harmony says gently. "I will help keep you safe.

"I don't think you can. He should still be in jail," I say.

"He is the one you told me about, right? The one who made you do those things with other kids then raped you," She asks.

"Yes. Why did she bring him here and how did she find me?" I asked myself aloud.

"I don't know love," Harmony answers even though I wasn't asking her. I wasn't asking anyone in particular. We heard the bikes in the distance. "They are back,"

"Please don't say anything yet," I beg. "You too Rider,"

"I'm not. You are. They need to know so they can protect you," Harmony ordered. "He said he wanted me, so I know that it's not over," I just nodded as Beast pulls Harmony out of the car.

"Are you okay?" Beast asks as he checks her for any marks. Harmony nods. "That is the guy we are watching. I got two other calls after you. Who is he?"

"Josie," Harmony orders in her authority voice.

"That is my mother and her pimp. He is the one who made me and other kids my age have sex on camera, then sold the tapes. He used to rape me before they took me away," I answer.

"You don't go off by yourself. If you have to work, then one of my brothers will go with you," Beast orders. "If it's okay with you Josie, I will tell my brothers, so they know those from whom we are protecting you from. I will tell your story but only because we have to protect you. Harmony is my life so that means you are protected too. It would hurt my woman if you got hurt,"

"Okay," I answer.

"That is settled," Beast says as he guides Harmony into the building. I follow behind them. He walks us both to their room. After we are safely inside, he locks the door. I glanced back.

"He does that to keep me safe," Harmony says. "Or should I say us now," She points at her belly.

"I'm glad you have someone," I say as my phone rings. I don't know the number, so I answer. "Hello,"

"Put it on speaker." She mouths. I do what she says.

"Josephine. I'm sorry but I had to give you up to say my child. She is too important to me to let him hurt," Donna says through the phone.

"She is too important, but I wasn't when I was a little girl?" I ask.

"I didn't want you. You were somebody else's child, and I didn't like you because he wanted you. You were never important. I got clean when they took you because I never loved you. You were the reason I was using," Donna says into the phone. Tears began to fall down my cheeks. Harmony snatched the phone out of my hand.

"You're a bitch. How bout we don't help you or your daughter?" Harmony says and hangs up the phone. The phone rings again. She picks it up and puts it on speaker. "You don't even have another daughter."

"Look here you stupid bitch. I'm going to make sure he rapes you then beats you until you can't move. We will make sure he rips your child out of you and does her like we did the other bitch with you."

"That is what you are going to let him do to me. Good luck. Eat a dick bitch and stop calling her," Harmony hangs up again. "I think it's time for you to change your number,"

"I don't even know how they got my number," I answer. She took my phone out of my hand and opened the back. She took the sim card out and broke it in two. "Why." I didn't understand what she was doing.

"If they know the right person, they can track you from it. I will get you a new phone. He is telling the truth with knowing people. I will not let my family get hurt. You are my family," She hugs me as she talks. "I heard what she said. You are important to me," She continues to hug me as we sit on the bed. We sit there for a little while before we hear the door unlocking.

"It's time we show you how to protect yourself," Beast says as he comes into the room. "Crazed is going to show you how to shoot a gun. We want you to be safe. One day you may need to know how,"

"Okay," I say and leave out of the room.

CHAPTER FOUR: HARMONY

Two Weeks Later,

It has been two weeks since we had a run in with the man who hurt my friend. I needed to get some things for the baby. "Jerome, I need to go to the store to get our babies some things," I say.

"Okay. Get dressed and we will go," Beast answers. I get dressed. Beast helps me put my shoes on. I follow him out of the room and into the bar.

"Beast we have a problem," One of the brothers said as he came running up. "We have been following this guy. We put a tracker on both guys but only one is working. We went to where the one was staying, and we found this," The guy shows him a picture.

"Go back to our room and stay there. We will go when I get back. Brink and Toast will stay with you," Beast says as he kisses me on my lips. "Brink, Toast," He yells.

"What's good?" Brink asks.

"I need you too to stay here and protect our families. Josie will be sent over to my room after I get Crazed," Beast says as he takes me into the room. "Tell all the other girls to stay locked in their rooms no matter what they hear. They are after our women not the sisters."

"You be careful. I love you," I say as I kiss him. He kisses me back. He puts his arms around me and pulls me close to him.

"I will be. I love you too. You stay in this room until I unlock it," Beast says as he leaves me. Five minutes later he opens the door and Josie walks in.

"What's going on?" I ask.

"I don't know," Josie answers. We sit on the bed, and I lay down to take a nap. I close my eyes and I'm asleep within seconds. That only lasts a few minutes because I'm woke up by the sound of gun shots.

"Get the girls somewhere safe. We can't let them get to Harmony," I hear one of the guys say. I pick up my phone and dial Beast's number.

"What's wrong?" Beast asks in the phone.

"Someone is here. I hear gun shots," I cry.

"Brink get up. Brink," I hear Toast say. "You son of a bitch,"

"Brink is hurt," I say.

"You need to hide," Beast orders. "I'm on my way. I love you,"

"I love you too," I reply.

"You girls need to hide," Toast says outside the door right before everything went silent. I can feel the tears rolling down my cheeks. There aren't many places to hide. We climb into the bathtub. I hear the door slam and we lay silent. Josie is crying now but I will not give anyone else the satisfaction of hurting me.

"If you want to live you need to come out of the bathroom now. I will shoot. One, two, three, Four," He counts.

"Okay, we are coming out," I say as we walk out.

"You have must be Josie. Man, you are beautiful," The guy says. "Let's go. He wants the both of you. Your pregnant. It's his baby right. I get you if I bring his Josephine to him," He points his gun at my belly.

"Okay. We will go peacefully," I say as I hold my hands up. Josie follows behind me. I will not be another victim. I walked out and saw my boys on the ground. Brink wasn't breathing but I could see that Toast was. I sent a prayer to him. We got in the back of a truck. He drove for a little while before we got to where we were going. It seemed like we left town. When we got there, he got us both out and walked us into the building.

"It's funny how you actually thought I couldn't get to you," The guy said as we walked inside the building. "I wish you would have just come with me. My little Josie. I lost a lot of money because of you,"

"Don't call me that. I'm not yours," Josie grated finding her voice. "I'm not afraid of you anymore." I knew she was. He backhanded her so hard that she fell to the ground. He knew too.

"Leave her alone you bastard," I said as I brought my elbow back and hit the guy holding me in the face. "Compensating for something limp dick," He points his gun at my belly.

"Watch your mouth you little bitch," The bastard said. "I own her. She is mine. Get up and clean yourself up. You over there come hold her and don't be stupid like him,"

"Bitch," The guy I hit said as he walked off. The bastard looked at one of the other guards and moved his head towards the guy I hit. The guy nodded and followed him. Five seconds later I heard a gunshot.

"You are whatever I say you are. You thought you got away didn't you. I have been looking for you since I got out," He said. "Bitch I own you. I made a lot of money off your movies. I still do and Tony misses you. He has grown up to so now we can make grown up movies,"

"You're sick," I say as he puts his attention on me.

"Yes, the beautiful pregnant woman. I got guys that like that kind of stuff. I could make some money off you," He says as he walks up to me. He takes his finger and moves it down my face. He continues down until he gets between my breasts. I bring my knee up and knee him in his balls. "Bitch," He gets up and pulls his hand back. He smacks my cheek so hard my head hits the guy's chest who is holding me.

"You want me not her. You can take me if you leave her out of it," Josie says as she stands up. "I'm the one you want,"

"Hold that thought," He said.

"I will do whatever you want as long as you let her go," Josie pleads. That pisses him off. He walks over to her and hits her in her face again. She falls to the ground. He starts to kick her in her stomach.

"Stop," I yell as I struggle with the guy holding me. His grip is strong.

"You," Kick, "will," kick, "do," kick, "what," kick, "I," kick "tell," kick, "you," kick, "to," kick, "do. You act like you have a choice anyway," He says as he bends down to grab her by her hair. He brings her closer to his face. "You belong to me,"

"Stop it you bastard. Leave her alone," I scream. He turns and looks at me. His smile is sinister. I can sense the evil coming off him heavily. He picks her up by the collar of her shirt and hits her until she slumps, and she looks dead. "Does it make you feel powerful putting your hands on a woman. Only pussies do things like that," He walks over to me and grabs my breast. I struggle to get his hands off of me which pisses him off more. He hits me again but this time he hits me like a guy. It hurt but I wasn't going to let him know that.

"Take the whore and this bitch in the same room. We leave in the morning," The bastard says.

"Okay Joseph," The guy who took us said as he pulled me towards the room. He puts me inside and leaves me there. Not long after he comes into the room holding Josie over his shoulder. He just throws her down on the bed. "Don't make no noise or he will hurt you," I see something in his eyes, I just don't know what it is. The guy he works for is crazy, so I don't know. I know my man will find me if it's the last thing he does. Josie moans. I go to her.

"I'm so sorry. Therefore, I wanted to leave you. I wanted to protect you," Josie whispered. I look at her and her face is swollen. "My ribs hurt," I make her stay in her spot, but I lay with her. I sing her to sleep. I lay there with my eyes open, and I say a prayer to my man that he gets to me in time to save us both. I don't know how long I laid there when I began to hear gun shots somewhere in the distance. I sat up and woke Josie. "What's going on?"

"I think our men have come to save us. I need you to try and get up. I help her out of the bed. "Can you walk enough to get ready to get out of here?" I ask.

"I can but you have to help me," Josie replies.

"I got you," I reply as I walk her towards the door. I don't hear any commotion, so I lean her against the wall. "I need you to stay here. I have to make sure it's safe for us to leave out of the room," She nods, and I slowly open the door. It was unlocked so I stuck my head out. I did not see anyone, so I went back to get Josie off the road. We left out of the room. We are moving slow, but I know that we have to be careful. We get to another door that looks like it goes outside. I hear gunshots coming from the other direction. The gun shots stop, and I hear footsteps, so I find a corner and hide Josie there. I get ready to fight when I hear my name.

"Harmony," My man yells.

"I'm here," I yell. "I need help with Josie," I see him come around the corner with Crazed and I get excited. I run to him, and he wraps me in his arms. "I knew you would find me," He looks me over. When he sees my bruised face, he gets piss. "Where is he?"

"He is gone now," Gorilla says. "He was pulling off when we got around the corner. I shot at him, but he got away,"

"I'm not letting you out of my sight until this bastard is caught," Beast answers

"Where is Josie?" Crazed asked.

"She's over here," I answer as I show him. He picks her up and carries her out. "Be careful he broke her ribs. He kicked her a lot. Get me out of here." I look at my man.

"We brought a truck. Let's go," Beast said as he helped me out of the building. When I get in the back seat with Beast. I dread asking about Brink and Toast. Crazed is in the back of the SUV holding Josie.

"What about Toast and Brink?" I ask.

"Brink is gone. Toast is the reason we got to you so fast. He played dead long enough to follow them. He was shot bad, but he will pull through. They shot Brink in the heart," Beast answers. I could tell he was pissed but he wanted to get me some where safe.

"Are the girls, okay? I fought back as much as I could. He kept pointing his gun at our baby. I broke one of the men's noses and the bastard shot him," I said as we drove the rest of the way to the club. When we got back Beast put me and Josie in our room with locked doors and left to have a meeting. As we walked past where Brink and Toast were shot, tears fell for one of my guys. He didn't deserve what happened to him. He died protecting me and my baby. I knew they were getting payback and I was glad. I wanted the bastards to pay.

CHAPTER FIVE: BEAST

It has been an uneventful two weeks since we had a run in with someone who is a threat to my woman and my brothers. It will hurt my woman if her friend gets hurt so I will do what I can to make sure it doesn't happen. She is my world, and I will do whatever it takes to make her happy. She is carrying my child, so it makes her more important than anyone else in this world. My brothers understand that so they do what they can to protect her. If anything happens to her because of Josie, then hell will be paid.

"Jerome, I need to go to the store to get our baby some things," Harmony says. She is the only one allowed to call me by my real name.

"Okay. Get dressed and we will go," I say. She gets dressed and I help her with her shoes. When we are done, I head out of the room. As soon as we walk into the bar Gunner came running up to me.

"Beast we have a problem," Gunner says. "We have been following this guy. We put a tracker on but only one is working. We went to where the one was staying, and we found this," Gunner shows me a picture of Josie and Harmony when they went to the store last week. While we were busy watching him, he had someone take a picture of them. In the back it shows Gorilla in the back watching them to keep them safe.

"Go back to our room and stay there. We will go when I get back. Brink and Toast will stay with you. Tell all the other girls to stay locked in their rooms no matter what," I order as I kiss my woman on her lips. I have to keep her safe. We have to move to find this guy. "Brink, Toast," I yell as I take her back into our room.

"You be careful. I love you," She says as she kisses me again. I kiss her back. I put my arm around her and pull her close to me.

"I will be. I love you too. You stay in this room until I unlock it," I order. I leave out and lock the door on my way out. I head straight to Crazed room. I knock on the door. "It's Beast open up now," Crazed opens the door.

"What's going on?" Crazed asked. I hand him the picture. "Where's Josie?"

"I'm here," Josie answers.

"Come on. I need you to stay with Harmony for a little while," I order and turn. I go to my room because I know that she is following me.

"What's going on?" Josie asks.

"I need you to be safe for Harmony. I don't have time to explain," I say as I unlock my door and push her in. I meet Harmony's eyes and smile. I need her safe. When I closed the door, I turned to Brink and Toast. "Thank you, brothers. She means the world to me. Keep my family safe,"

"We got you brother. She is family to us too," Brink says as I leave. The rest of the club get on our bikes and go to the last place we know where he was. When we get there Crow and Bear are waiting on us. I called Tattoo.

"Are you still on the brother?" I ask.

"Yeah. He has been in the same spot all night. We are at his house," Tattoo says.

"Stay on him," I order.

"Okay. What's going on?" Tattoo asks.

"The one slipped past our guys. They found a picture of the women and Gorilla protecting them. He is getting ready to do something I just don't know what yet. Hold on my phone is ringing," I say as I look at my phone. It's Harmony. "It's Harmony holds on," I click over. "What's wrong?"

"Someone is here. I hear gun shots," She cries. I'm pissed now but I don't need her to hear it in my voice.

"Brink get up. Brink," Toast yells. "You son of a bitch." I can hear the gun shots though the phone.

"Brink is hurt," She says.

"You need to hide," I order. "I'm on my way. I love you,"

"I love you too," I reply.

"You girls need to hide," Toast says as I'm hanging up the phone.

"We need to go now," I say as I run to my bike. I hear my brothers follow my lead. I rush back to the club. By the time we get there the girls are gone, and I rush through the building to my room. When I get there Brink is lifeless in a pool of blood. His sister is holding him and crying. Toast isn't anywhere in the club house. I touch her shoulder as Doc helps her up. I search the room.

"Where are they?" Crazed asked.

"I don't know," I answer. Just then my phone rings. "Hello,"

"Beast. It's Toast. I played dead long enough to follow them. I know where they are. I don't know how much time I have left since I lost a lot of blood. We are right outside of town. Go towards Indiana and right before you go across state lines there is a road. I need help," Toast said.

"Hang on," I say. "He is trying to tell us how to get there but I don't think I understand. He is bleeding out, he needs us."

"I know how to track his phone. Hang on," Gunner says then goes into the office. Five minutes later he stands up. "It's on your phone now,"

"Let's suit up and ride," I say as we go to our guns in the shed. I grab a nine mil and an AK47. We got them just for this. I fill a bag up with some smoke bombs and grenades. Hawk takes a sniper rifle out and I just look at him. I know he was sniper in the marines. I'm glad he is on our side.

"We are ready," Gorilla said.

"I cleaned up Brink. He is in the kitchen on the table. I covered him up. Let's get these bastards," Doc said as he got on his bike. "Tamyry is in the room with Tammy and Bridgette." I nod my head.

"I know we are hurting right now. I'm pissed too. Let's show these fuckers what it feels like when you mess with one of ours," I say as they all get on their bikes to find Toast. I get in the SUV with Crazed and Gorilla. It took us one hour to get there. Toast was barely holding on. When we get to him, he is barely able to stand straight. "Take care of him Doc. We got this,"

"Give them hell," Doc says as he makes Toast lay down so he can bandage him up.

"Brink," Toast asks. Doc shakes his head.

"Stay here. I'm going to high ground. Give me three seconds," Hawk says and takes off in the opposite direction than where we are going. Five seconds later I receive a text message saying ready. We head down to the front but right before we get there the guy is already dead. Hawk cleared the way for us. Someone comes out to check on their guys and spots us. He shoots at Crazed and missed because Popeye pushed him out of the way. I tell Gunner, Tank, and Gorilla to go around the back. They head that way. I shoot the guy in the chest, and he falls. That is when the firefight started. Some other guys come to the door and start shooting. We hide behind some trees, so they don't get us too. We are shooting for another ten minutes before all the shooting stops by the door.

"Crazed, Knuckles, Crash with me. The rest stay out here just in case we miss the girls. Or if we miss someone," I order. Crazed, Knuckles and Crash followed me in through the door. The first guy hits the ground as Knuckles slipped his arm around his neck until he passed out. As Knuckles was laying him on the grown another guy came around the corner and I pointed my gun at his head. "Where are they?"

"GO TO HELL!!!" The guy said.

"That is where you're going if you don't tell me what I want to know," I grated.

"Fuck you," he said. "She is dead. After I ripped your child out of her stom…" He didn't get to finish his sentence because I put a bullet right between his eyes. I looked at him and went to find my woman. When I saw that all the bad guys were dead, I searched for her throughout the building.

"Harmony," I yell.

"I'm here," She yells. "I need help with Josie," I see her when I round the corner. She wobbles over to me. She falls in my arms. "I knew you would find me," I look her over. She has a bruise on the side of her face. "Where is he?"

"He is gone now," Gorilla says as he comes around the corner. "He was pulling off when we got around the back. I shot at him, but he got away.

"I'm not letting you out of my sight until this bastard is caught," Beast says.

"Josie?" Crazed asked.

"She's over here," Harmony answers as she shows her to us. Crazed picks her up and carries her out. "Be careful he broke her ribs. He kicked her a lot. Get me out of her." She looks at me with pain and tears. I know she is hurting.

"We brought a truck. Let's go," I said as I helped my woman out of the building. When she gets in the back of the truck she speaks. Crazed is holding Josie in the back.

"What about Toast and Brink?" She asks.

"Brink is gone. Toast is the reason we got to you so fast. He played dead long enough to follow them. He is bad off, but he will pull through. They shot Brink in the heart," I answer as we pull up by doc. I'm pissed but I need to get her home safely. He nods his approval. Toast is okay.

"Are the girls, okay?" Harmony asks and I nod. "I fought back as much as I could. He kept pointing his gun at our baby. I broke one of the men's noses and the bastard shot him." We drove the rest of the way to the club. When we got back, I escorted her back to the room and Crazed laid Josie in the bed. I locked the door so we could have a meeting. I could tell that it hurt her to see where Brink and Toast was shot protecting her. I could feel her pain, but I turned that into anger because that bastard will pay. Brink didn't deserve something so final, and I can't mourn for him until we get the people responsible. I head into our meeting room.

CHAPTER SIX: CRAZED

We went into the meeting room and sat in our seats. I could tell Beast has a heavy heart because I do too. "Let's take a moment of silence for our fallen brother," Beast says as we bow our heads for our moment of silence. We sit that way for five minutes. "First order of business, we find this bastard," Beast stops to control his anger. "The bastard bruised my woman's face. He raped Josie when she was a child. He killed one of our brothers. He has to die. Call your brother-in-law and give him the guy's picture."

"I have this army friend who wants to move here and help. We served together. He saved my life in Iraq," Hawk said. "Brink was my brother. This guy will not slip through our fingers,"

" I will. He is on his way here now. He text me as soon as we got back. He has a small team ready to help," Monster said. "He is trustworthy, and he is willing to help. FBI gets credit for the bust, but we get to help. He already cleared it with his boss. This is him," He pauses and looks at me.

"Answer," Beast says.

"Hello. You have a name for me. See you in the morning," Monster says then hangs up.

"What's up?" Beast asks.

"He says it's bad. That guy is on the FBI most wanted list. He is a sex trafficker. He's wanted regarding at least ten kids that they know of," Monster answers. "They took Tony Wilkerson twenty-five years ago. He would be the same age as the girls,"

"I can't stand scum like that," Gorilla said.

"We have some extra rooms for the agents and for your army friend," Beast said. "I will not rest till we catch both. Any more business before I go check on my woman. I need to make sure her and my kid are okay."

"I'm good," I say.

"Meeting adjourned," Beast says. We pile out of church. I followed Beast while the rest of the club got ready to guard our family. "You need to stay with Josie. I know you don't believe you deserve love, but you do. You need to forgive yourself brother. Toya wasn't your fault. You were a child too. Life is too short."

"Damn she made you soft," I countered.

"No not soft. She gave me something to live for. She gave me something to fight for. She is special. My angel," Beast answered as he opened the door to his room. The girls were laying in the bed. Harmony was staring at the wall singing to Josie. "Hey, beautiful." She looks up at him with tears in her eyes. She put her finger to her lips.

"I'm going to take her to my room," I whispered. Harmony nodded her head. I picked up Josie and carried her to my room laying her down in the bed once we got there.

"Stay with me please," She asks. I covered her up and laid beside her. She cuddled into my side. I wrapped my arms around her. "I'm safe here," She put her hand on my chest where my heart is. "My hero," Then she goes back to sleep. I know she is just saying that now. How can she love someone who couldn't even protect his own sister. "Will you tell me about Toya?" She looks up at me and I couldn't say no. I thought she was asleep.

"She was five when he first started having sex with her," I whispered. It hurt my heart talking about it. I knew I needed to open up to her.

"How old were you?" She asked softly.

"Seven," I answered. "When she turned eight and I was ten I lost her. I couldn't stand her cries, so I left her there with him. I just left her there. I met

Jerome and Damien at the park. Every time it started; I left her there. How could I just leave my little sister to him. Our mother was a crack head whore who was never home anyway. When I got back to the house, she was in the corner crying. She was sitting in a pile of her own blood and feces. We never had warm water, so I had to warm up majority of the water for the tub," I stop and look at her. She touches my cheek with the palm of her hand. It makes my heart hurt a little less.

"It's okay. I'm right here," She answered.

"While I cleaned her up, she begged me to take her out of the world. I was too selfish to let her go. I cleaned her bed sheets and dressed her. After I laid her in her clean sheets, I took a cold shower to form a plan. After all her blood and feces went down the drain, I had a plan. He always kept his gun on his hip. He was a police officer. I fell asleep but was woke up by her crying. I grabbed a chair to stop him long enough to get his gun," I stopped for a second. I took a deep breath. This is extremely hard to talk about. I tightened my grip on her.

"It's okay. I'm not going anywhere. Ever," Josie says.

"After I hit him, he started beating me up. Right before I passed out, I heard the gun shot. He fell on top of me. I'm struggling to push him off. I'm looking at her. She looks me in the eyes. She tells me I deserve the best and to be happy. No, I don't. She tells me it's not my fault, but she can't take the pain. I beg. No, I yell. She looks at me with pain and sadness in her eyes. There is no innocence left. No more light, no more joy. Only despair and pain remain. She pulls the trigger. I see her brains behind her. I hold her in my arms crying," I stop looking in the distance.

"Stay with me Deiondre," Josie whispers as she puts both hands on my face. "Look at me,"

"I don't want to let go of my sister. Why didn't they come sooner? I know they heard her scream and cries. They could have saved her. I should have saved her. I asked them. They didn't have an answer. The tears stopped at the hospital. Anger and guilt followed in its wake," I say as I look into her eyes. "I see the same thing in your eyes. Pain and self-hatred,"

"It wasn't your fault. You were a child too," Josie says as she moves her thumbs back and forth. It soothes me. I understand what my and brother feels.

"It wasn't yours either," I counter.

"What could make a mother not want her child? Why even have that child?" She asks.

"I'm glad our mothers did," I said as I tightened my hold on her. "Tell me your story."

"I was three when she first took me to work with her. She was a prostitute. She sat me on the corner. Her favorite words for me were slut, whore, and bitch. I still don't understand how a three-year-old could be a slut, whore, or bitch. She's three," She stops and closes her eyes. She is still having trouble breathing. She smiles at me. "For two years he gave me to other kids. Some my age others were older, much older. Tony did it to me the most. He was a few years older than me. He acted like he like it. It hurt terribly."

"Look at me. You are here with me," I say as I make her look at me.

"I was five when he decided I was old enough for him. It hurt the worst. After that first time he came for me every night. After he finished, he took me with him to his house. I remember the first time he had sex with me. My mother watched to make sure I did what he wanted. She even told me to shut up and do what I'm told. That day he left me at home. She waited for me to finish my shower. She wouldn't let me have a towel but if the floor got wet, she would beat me. Air drying in the bathroom shower helped a little. When I got to my room, she beat me for fifteen minutes. I still love her though," She says. "It went on for three more years before the police took me from there. I met Harmony. She stopped two girls from beating me up," She laughs. "The first and only person to stand up for me,"

"I can see it. She is fiercely protective and loyal. She is something else," I laugh.

"She is my light in the dark. She brings joy to anyone she meets," She says.

"I believe it. She put a spell on Beast. She is the only one besides me that calls him Jerome. I can't hide my feelings from you anymore. I fell in love with you, but I still don't believe I deserve it," I say.

"I fell for you but to protect you he can't know. He will directly come after you. I can't lose you like you lost Brink. He was my friend too," She said. "He isn't finished. Now he wants Harmony too so he can break her like he broke me years ago,"

"You're not broken," I say. "Let's get some rest," She nods, and I hold her close. We fall asleep within seconds.

CHAPTER SEVEN: JOSIE

Three weeks Later

It's been three weeks and we haven't heard from the bastard from my nightmares. I know it's not over, but I also know that he is planning something. The club has been busy. Monster's sister and her husband have been down here with his team. There are four people all together including the brother and his wife. Two women and two men. I don't talk to any of them because I stay in my room. They have his picture, and they have his fingerprints. They went back to the old school they were holding us at for all the fingerprints, so they have names. I just wish this could all be over.

"Josie come on," Harmony said outside my door.

"I'm coming," I replied. I had just woken up.

"I'm hungry come on," She wines as I'm opening the door. Tank was standing guard. She is used to it, but I'm not. I followed her to the kitchen. "Where is Jerome?"

"He is talking to Monster," Tank answered.

"He's in with my brother and husband," Monsters sister-in-law said as she came into the room. "Hey little baby," She is sweet. She spends a lot of time with me and Harmony.

"I'm here love," Beast says as he comes into the room.

"I was hungry, so Tank walked with me," Harmony says with her happy dance. Everyone laughed. "What?"

"You are too cute," Monster's sister-in-law said.

"Thank you, Layla," Harmony replied. I watch Beast pull Harmony on his lap as he sat down. He starts rubbing her belly. "I missed you," She kisses him. Crazed comes in the kitchen and stops in front of me.

"I'm going into town for tonight. We are going to have a cookout for everyone staying her at the compound. We have a lot of people to feed," Crazed asked. "Do you want to come?"

"Yes, I do. Do you need anything?" I ask Harmony.

"Some Oreos, chocolate ice cream and jalapeno cheddar Cheetos," Harmony answered. "Baby I want to lay down. Will you come lay with me?"

"Yeah beautiful. Let's go," Beast says as he gets up. He picks her up in his arms.

"I can walk stallion," Harmony says as he carries her to their room. I shake me Head.

"Are they always like that?" Layla asks.

"Always. I'm glad she is happy. She deserves it," I reply.

"So do you," Layla says.

"You ready?" Crazed asks. I nod. We leave and get in an SUV. We drive to the store. As we are shopping, I notice that someone is following us. I grab Crazed hand.

"Can I have a hug?" I ask. He looks at me like I lost my mind but when he saw my eyes he leaned in and hugged me. "Someone is following us. Behind us at the cereal. I watched him leave from in front of the compound and then I see him now," I whisper.

"Keep shopping. I'm going to run to the SUV. I have my gun. Where is your purse. Put this in there," Crazed whispers and hands me a gun. I do what I'm told. "I forgot my money. I will be right back," I nod and continue to walk around. He goes out to the SUV. I don't know what he is doing but I trust him. I get everything that we need when Crazed comes back in.

We get our things and I notice the guy is still following us. He gets two people behind us. We buy our things and go to the car. After everything is done Crazed puts me in the car then leaves me there. I don't know what he is doing but I wait on him.

I'm sitting in the SUV for a little while before Crazed comes back. He hands me a piece of paper that has numbers and letters on it. "The license plates?" I ask.

"Yeah," Crazed answers. We go back to the compound and take everything inside. The guys helped. "Put everything up and I will be right back," He leaves me for a little while before he comes back with Monster and his brother-in-law. Layla helped me put everything up.

"Hey beautiful," Layla's husband says as he hugs her.

"Did you get a name Jayden," Layla asks.

"Yeah. The car is registered to Tony Wilkerson," Jayden answers.

"That's the kid that has been missing for a long time right," Layla asked.

"Yeah," Jayden's partner said as he came into the kitchen.

"Okay," Layla said. "I work for the FBI too. I'm a cyber analysist,"

"Cool. Can you search for a Donna Wright and see if she even has a daughter?" I ask.

"Who is she?" Jayden asks.

"She is my mother. She told him where I was. She said she didn't have a choice, but I don't believe her. She is the one that gave me to him when I was three," I answered.

"Seriously," Layla asks.

"Yes," I answer.

"It will be my pleasure to bring her down too," Layla grated. "I will be in the office we are using," She leaves us there.

"She takes things that happen to kids to the heart. Her best friend's daughter was taken last year. When they found the little girl, she had been raped and murdered. She was two," Jayden says as he fixes him something to eat.

"We have it. We know his name," The female FBI agent said coming into the room.

"Good Job Rebecca. Thomas grabs everyone and get them in the party hall. We have to tell everyone what we know," Jayden said as he turned to go check on his wife.

"You want to go grab Beast and Harmony," Crazed said turning to me.

"Yeah," I say as I head to my best friend. I knock on the door.

"In a minute," Beast says.

"It's important. They have something," I say through the door.

"We're coming," Beast says.

"We're meeting in the party hall," I reply and leave to find Crazed. He is standing by Gorilla. I go over to him. "Hey,"

"How are you feeling?" Gorilla asked.

"I will feel better when this scumbag is caught," Crazed answered.

"Yeah. I can't stand people like him. How are you, Josie?" Gorilla replies. Everyone made it into the room.

"I'm okay. Will be better when I'm not scared anymore." I answer.

"I bet," Gorilla replied.

"If you can have a seat then take a seat," Jayden said. I looked around and saw Beast sitting with Harmony in his lap. "The guy we are looking for is Joseph Harris. He is a sex trafficker who has taken over a dozen kids. He has been on the most wanted list for years. He has a team of men working for him, but his right-hand man is Tony Wilkerson. He was three when they took him. That makes him twenty-eight," Jayden says.

"He feeds off being control over these kids. We have found every kid taken in the dark web. He collaborates with Donna Wright, known as Tammy Davison," Layla says. I look at her. Crazed wraps his arms around me. I felt tears falling. I looked at Harmony and I could tell she wanted to come to me. Layla looked at me with sadness in them. I knew then that she was going to tell me later.

"We are still looking for him. We need you to use the buddy system. I know you all are grown. To stay safe don't leave without at least two people. If you're not in the club have someone that is with you. This guy is ruthless and uncaring. He takes kids and does with them what he wants so he can get rich," Rebecca said.

"If you see anything then let us know. We are searching for this guy. If you need more information then come talk to Rebecca, Layla, Jayden, or me," Thomas said.

"That is all for now. We will be here until this guy is caught," Jayden said. Crazed held onto me until everyone went their separate ways. Beast, Harmony, Crazed and I followed Layla and Jayden. "Come in and have a seat. This is serious,"

"I'm listening," I said.

"Okay. A long time ago a program was made that took every missing child and showed what they would look like as an adult. First, we looked up Donna Wright, it came up as an alias for a woman from

Delaware. She never had a child. She is in our database for kidnapping two other kids that we know of. She was a babysitter for twins. When she disappeared so did the twins. She wasn't your mother. You were taken from your parents when you were three months old," Layla said.

"I have parents that wanted me?" I asked as Harmony came to hold me. "Where are they? Can I meet them? Have they been looking for me this whole time?"

"This is the hard part. They were killed so the person could take you. We don't know who killed them, but I'm guessing it was Donna," Jayden said.

"Was Donna really a crackhead?" I ask.

"She was, but she moved around with Joseph. He waited until the kids were old enough to take from her. She oversaw raising the kids until they were of age," Thomas said. "I'm so sorry," I felt tears falling.

"At least I can believe that they loved me," I said.

"I'm here for you," Harmony says.

"I know," I answer. They stood around talking for a few more minutes before I dismissed myself and went to bed. My head was spinning, and I needed some rest. It took me a long time to fall into a deep sleep.

******

I thought everyone in the club was sleeping when I was laying in the bed by myself. I opened my eyes to find I was alone. I had decided earlier tonight that I was going to run to keep her safe. Harmony is my best friend and I know that he will try to get her if I don't leave. I know that it hurt her when she thought that I was leaving. She is the greatest person I know, and she will sacrifice herself to keep me safe. I packed a bag and walked out of his room. I'm going to miss him, but I know that everyone is safer without me.

I went towards the front peeking around the corner to make sure no one would see me. Loud music still playing. I decided to go out the back. Warm air hits my face right outside of the door. "Are you sneaking away in the middle of the night?" I heard a deep voice ask. I turned and watched as Gorilla came out of the shadows. "You know that it's going to hurt Harmony if you leave?"

"I know but I feel this is the only way to keep her safe," I answer. "She already came close to getting hurt because of me. Brink is dead because of me,"

"Are you sure about that? It wasn't your fault that Brink got killed. That bastard is the blame. We would never let anything happen to her or you. Beast will kill anyone that threatens his woman. You don't know where most of these guys come from," Gorilla countered.

"Tell Harmony I love her please. I have to go," I replied and left him standing there. "You guys don't know him like I do," I mumbled to myself. He will use these people against me. I got in my car and drove out of the complex. I didn't look back. The tears fell as I drove away. I was driving for about an hour before my phone rang. I picked up my phone. "I know you're mad. I had to protect you,"

"You don't need to protect her. That is my job. You should have stayed put," Beast said.

I need you to come back," Crazed begged. "I can't protect you if you are gone. I have to protect you. I'm in love with you."

"I'm sorry. Harmony, I want you to know I love you. Beast take care of her and my God children. Crazed I know you didn't want me to get attached to you but if you never hear from me again, I want you to know that I fell in love with you. You deserve love. I know you saw your sister when you looked at me and I'm sorry for bringing you pain," I said as somebody ran into the back of my car. I looked in the rearview mirror and saw a SUV. "Stop," My phone fell on the ground. They hit me one more time and my car flipped. It flipped four times before I lost consciousness.

CHAPTER EIGHT: CRAZED

The partying isn't what it used to be since I had Josie for the first time. I do my best to stay away from her. It's getting harder every day. I want her so bad that it hurts my heart. I know she isn't my sister and I'm glad, but I still see my sisters vacant eyes all the time. When Layla was telling her about her mother, I wanted to hold her. I can't believe that she was kidnapped as a kid. I was holding her when everyone was being briefed. When she tried to leave a few weeks ago it pissed me off. When she was kidnapped, I knew I wouldn't be able to stay away from her too long. I down my drink and get up from the bar. "Where are you going?" My brother asked.

"I'm done for the night. I'm going to check on Josie," I answered.

"Why do you keep playing the fence with her?" My brother asked.

"What?" I growled.

"We all know you want her. She wants you. What is the problem?" He asked.

"She reminds me of Toya Monster," I answered.

"You do know that she isn't Toya. She is stronger. I don't want to make you mad but I'm just making a point. Josie made it," Monster said.

"I know. I just can't get my sister out of my head," I answered. I leave him there and go to my room. I softly open the door but when I see she isn't there I get pissed. I go straight to Beast room. I bang on the door.

"My woman is sleeping so this better be good," Beast growls from inside the door. When he swings the door open, he is butt ass naked. I don't pay him any mind. I'm used to it. "What do you want Jackass?" He is surprised when he sees me.

"Josie isn't in here, is she?" I asked.

"What? She's not in your room," Harmony asks as she sits up.

"I went to my room to check on her and she was gone," I answered.

"Shit. She's running," Harmony says.

"What baby?" Beast asks as he turns and looks at her.

"Get dressed please," Harmony says as she looks at my brother. "Close the door. I need to put my clothes on," He closed the door, and I heard commotion from behind the door. "I knew she was going to do it. She is so damn hardheaded. I told her she was safer here, but she does what she wants,"

"I know boo," Beast says.

"She is going to get herself killed," Harmony says.

"Calm down. Let's get out there and see if we can find her," Beast says to Harmony. They walk out of the room a few minutes later. I follow them out into the party. He looks at one of our brothers and makes a cut with his hand. When the music stopped everyone turned to Beast. "Anyone seen Josie?"

"Yeah. I saw her as she was leaving," One of my brothers yelled. He walked up to us.

"Let's go where we hold church so we can talk," Beast says. "You guys can go back to partying," We head into where we hold church. Beast sat at the head of the table, and he pulled Harmony on his lap. He wrapped his arms around her and let his hands rest on her belly. "Tell us everything Gorilla,"

"I was outside checking the perimeter. I saw her coming out of the back door. I walked up to her. I told her that she knew that it was going to hurt you. Well, I said Harmony. She said she knew but it was the only way to keep her and the baby safe. I asked her if she was sure about that. I told her that we would never let anything happen to her. I let her know you would kill anyone that hurt or even threatened your woman. She doesn't know but most of us came from broken homes. She said to tell Harmony that she loves her. She left after that. Before she left, she said we don't know him like she does. She didn't think I heard that last part, but I did," Gorilla answered.

"Why didn't you try harder to stop her?" Beast asked.

"He couldn't have stopped her. She is stubborn like that," Harmony said as she pulled out her phone and dialed Josie's number. She put it on speaker.

"I know you are mad. I had to protect you," Josie said.

"You don't need to protect her. That is my job. You should have stayed put," Beast says.

"I need you to come back," I said. "I can't protect you if you are gone. I have to protect you. I'm in love with you,"

"I'm sorry. Harmony, I want you to know I love you. Beast take care of her and my God children. Crazed I know you did not want me to get attached to you but if you never hear from me again, I want you to know that I fell in love with you. You deserve love. I know you saw your sister when you looked at me and I'm sorry for bringing you pain," Josie says as we heard something loud. "Stop," It sounded like the phone hit the floorboard.

"Josie," Harmony yells. "You have to go save her," Harmony begins to cry. "Hurry," We stopped talking for a few minutes. We could hear other voices. I muted the phone and pushed record.

"Joseph and Donna said not to hurt her. Tony said he wanted to see her. Damn it she is unconscious. Leave everything. It's going to take at least thirty minutes to get back to them," A deep voice says.

"You know he wanted the other one too," Another voice says.

"Yeah, but I don't think he is going to let the pregnant one out of his sight. They moved all the families closer to them. You see the girl at the diner. I wanted her but they moved her too fast," The deep voice says.

"Yeah. Let's get her back to him. He has big plans for her. She might be out for the whole trip but still give her this," The other says. We hear doors closed. It sounded like a truck. The engine was loud. Beast had left out of the room to get Layla and Jayden.

"What's going on?" Layla asks.

"Josie left. We were talking to her when it sounded like someone running her off the road. We heard them talking. Harmony recorded them talking. We have to find where she wrecked," I said.

"Okay let's track where her phone is," Jayden said as he left out of the room.

"We are going to find her," Layla said as she wrapped her arm around Harmony who was crying hard.

"I got her," Beast said as he came and held his woman. I wanted so bad to hold mine too. I promised that when we find her, I will never let her go again. She will be mine.

"We found it. Let's go," Jayden said as we left.

"I'm staying here to protect my family. Find your girl," Beast said to me. I left with the agents. When we got there, they called in the local CSI to hurry up the process. They took everything collected to the Lab. Layla went with the rest of her team to the local police station. As soon as they got the lab results, they came back to the club.

"We have what we need. It's a 2007 Chevy Silverado, Gray," Layla said as Agent White pulled up traffic cam recordings for the time of the accident. They followed them until they came to a warehouse. "That is where they are. I only need four of you. Hawk since you have military experience. Jay, we need you. Crazed, I know you won't sit back so get ready. Tank and Gorilla we need you too,"

"I'm coming too," Toast said as he came up. "For Brink. They almost ended me,"

"Okay," Layla replied.

"The rest of us will stay back and protect our families," Beast replied.

"We have to take him alive. I have the swat team meeting us there," Jayden said. "We need to go before they move her," We got in the SUV the FBI brought with them and headed to the warehouse. When we got there, we parked back some. We knew they were in there because the truck was there. There were a few other expensive vehicles. FBI and swat went in. Tank, Gorilla, Hawk, Toast, and I went in after. We moved behind the FBI as they cleared the whole warehouse. They killed at least seven men, stopping the other three including Joseph. Donna wasn't with the guys. I went through a few doors and found Josie. She was still passed out on the floor. I checked her over. She had some bruises and scrapes but other than that she looked beautiful. I picked her up. I didn't understand why he became so careless. He has been getting away with it for years, but he wanted her so bad that didn't care what happened.

When I carried her outside there were kids and young girls everywhere. I saw them hand cuff Josie's fake mother. I want to hurt her for what she did to my woman. I knew now that I was going to have to claim her or let her go. I think I will choose to keep her. I got in one of the SUVs with my brothers and we went back to our club. Harmony was waiting on us when we got back. "I will let them tell you everything. I need to get her to bed so she can wake up to safety. I will be with her until she wakes up," Harmony nodded, and I took her to the room. I don't know how long I laid holding her when I slowly drifted off to sleep.

CHAPTER NINE: JOSIE

I woke up in Deiondre's arms and was confused. The last thing I remembered was someone running me off the road. I sat up quickly. Deiondre stirred beside me. "Are you okay?" He asked.

"Harmony?" I asked.

"She is with Beast," He answered.

"What happened?" I asked.

"We got them both. They will not hurt you again. We can put your past behind you," He answered.

"I wish you could put yours behind you too," I whispered.

"I'm working on that. I want to be with you. You just have to be patient with me. I can't tell you that I won't push you away ever again, but I will try. Just don't give up on me," He countered.

"I could say the same. I know that I want to be with you," I replied. He did something I have been waiting for since the last time. He laid me down and made love to me. It was the best thing I have ever felt in my life. He went slow and we spent the rest of the night pleasing each other. After hours of pleasure, we laid in each other's arms and fell into a deep sleep.

******

I was aroused out of my sleep by the sound of someone knocking on the door. "I know you are in there," My best friends voice came through the door.

"Give me a minute," I said as I untangled mine and Deiondre's legs. I put his shirt on and went to the door. I stepped out and Harmony didn't have a pleasant look on her face.

"I could kill you for making me stress like that," Harmony says as she pulls me into a hug. "Don't ever scare me like that again,"

"I won't I promise. Deiondre said they got them," I answered.

"They did. I'm glad you are safe now. I wanted to ask you. Will you be my maid of honor?" She asked.

"Of course," I answer.

"You set a date," I asked.

"Yes. Two months from now. It's going to be in the party hall. This weekend we are going to pick out our dresses. I'm going to ask Bridgette to be a bridesmaid. I need three more," She answered.

"When you wake up, we can go shopping. Of course, Beast will be there with me. He still will not let me leave his sight. He is so protective of me. It gets old sometimes, but I love him for it," Harmony says. "Go lay back down," She leaves me standing there. I go back into the room. Crazed is looking at me with his Chestnut eyes.

"Do you want to get dressed and go?" Crazed said.

"No," I say as I climb on top of him. He puts his hands on each side of my hips. He is naked and all I have on is his shirt, so I feel his dick on my pussy. I can feel him getting hard as I grind up and down on him. I guide him inside of me and we make love. We kiss as he puts me in five distinct positions. We both organism and then lay down. He wraps his arms around me for a little while before we got up and got in the shower. I got on my knees and made him happy. He lifted me against the shower and made me organism again. When we were both sated, we washed each other up. We finished and both of us got dressed. We headed into the kitchen looking for Harmony and Beast since that is her favorite spot in the whole building. In her defense she is eating for two now.

"Josie boo!" Harmony said when she saw me. She wiggled her hips in a funny way. "Finally. I'm happy for you too. You both deserve the best,"

"Thanks. Beast what's going on?" Crazed asked.

"Nothing trying to get my woman to listen. She just won't," Beast answers. "Harmony sits down," Harmony did one more move then sat on his lap.

"Daddy why do you always try to boss me around," She asked.

"Try is the key word. You just don't listen to me at all," Beast answers as he pulls her in for a kiss. They are so cute together.

"You knew she was crazy when you started talking to her," I said laughing at the face she is making. "What? You know I love you," She pokes her bottom lip out. "Are you ready to go?"

"Yes. Are you still coming?" She asked.

"Yes. Let me grab some money," Beast answers.

"You do know that when I get my dress you can't come with me. You can't see it until the wedding day," Harmony said as she got out of his lap.

"Until then I'm your shadow woman," Beast says as he leaves the kitchen for a few minutes.

"Are you coming too?" Harmony asked Crazed.

"Yeah," Crazed answered.

"Good. It's a double date," Harmony says wiggling her eyebrows. That little thing only she does right. I shake my head at her.

"I'm ready," Beast says as he smacks her ass. She smiles. We head out of the club and go to the shopping Centre in the middle of town. We shop for about four hours until Harmony said she was done. She looks closer to having this baby than she did yesterday. We got most of the things she needed for her wedding and the bridal shower. It's something I have to plan, and we are going to have fun. We don't have many friends, but the guys have sisters and Monsters wife is good with us. We get back to the club. Beast and Crazed carried all the bag in and put them where they went. "We are having a BBQ tonight. We deserve it with all the things we have been going through lately. Gorilla, Knuckles and Eagle go to the store. We need meat, sides, and drinks,"

"I want juice," Harmony says.

"We got you. What kind of juice you want?" Knuckles asked.

"Apple juice and Orange Juice," Harmony answers.

"Get some ribs and whatever else you decide you want. Make sure you grab some potato salad. We can set everything up while you are gone," Beast said.

"Okay," Gorilla says. They get in the SUV and go to the store.

"Let's get the grill and tables set up for the food," Beast orders and everyone gets to work. "You ladies sit down at the bar while we get everything together,"

"Yes Sir," Harmony says.

"I got your sir," Beast says. We watch as the guys get to work.

"Spill," Harmony orders.

"He decided that he didn't want to stay away from me anymore. Oh Harmony. I have never been in love, but I'm with him. It's like God made me just for him. He is still broken and so am I. We decided that we wanted to be broken together. I believe that will heal us both," I answered.

"I'm happy for you two. Neither one of you are broken. You just lost your way somehow. He really is a great guy," Harmony says as I look at him. He means the world to me and has for a while now.

"You look at him how I look at Beast. We have our hands full with those two. I wouldn't have it any other way. He really is different with me than he is with anyone. I see it. He is still rugged and ruff, but he is mine," She says.

"I have known Beast for a long time, and he has never been the way he is with you with anybody else," The bartender said.

"Seriously Kathy," I asked.

"Yes," Kathy answered.

"Diva makes sure the bar is fully stocked for tonight. We are celebrating," Beast said as he came to give Harmony a kiss. "What are you ladies gossiping about?"

"You," Harmony says. "I love you," She kisses him, and he leaves us there. The look on his face is priceless. She has him wrapped.

"He really loves you. I think you both deserve to be happy," Diva said as she left us sitting there.

"He feels the same way about you. I see it in the way he looks at you. He follows your every move. Look he is looking at you now," Harmony says as Crazed looks at me. Emeralds meet Chestnuts. He gives me that dashing smile and my heart melts. "See. You will be walking down the aisle at my wedding with him. Beast is supposed to ask him while they are setting everything up. All the guys are in our wedding too. I don't have that many friends, but I have to make sure they are all included,"

"You will. We will figure it out," I reply.

"Hey girls," One of the club girls walks up. I don't think she is so much of a whore but just wants to be around people. She is cool.

"Hey Sofia. I know they call you what they do but I don't like nicknames. It's so impersonal," Harmony says.

"It's all good. Knuckles gave me my nickname," She answered.

"You have a thing for Knuckles don't you," Harmony said.

"You don't miss a thing, do you?" Sofia asked.

"She doesn't," I answer for Harmony.

"It's a gift and a curse. What is your story?" Harmony asks.

"Don't mind her. She is great at reading people, but she meddles a lot too.

"No, I don't," Harmony answers offended.

"It's okay. Long story short. I was raped when I was sixteen by my next-door neighbor. He lied about it of course. He used a condom, so they didn't get any semen out of me. I was a virgin then. I didn't trust men after that. Me and Angel were friends since we were young. She told me about this place. At first, I was scared to come around. She was sleeping with all the men, but I just wanted someone to love. The first time I saw Knuckles I knew he was the one. He is the only one I have ever slept with here.

"I noticed. All the other girls throw themselves at the men but not you," Harmony says.

"You are very perceptive," Sofia replied.

"I'm here if you need someone," Harmony says.

"Me too," I say.

"You are going to have your hands full with the baby," Sofia said.

"It takes a village to raise a child," Harmony answers. "Would you like to be a bridesmaid, Sofia?"

"I would be honored," Sofia answers.

"Kathy, would you like to be one?" Harmony asked. "My sister is going to be one. I invited my mother. I have been talking to her. I forgave her,"

"I would be honored," Kathy answered.

"They are moving up here to be closer to me. I think it will be good for me and my sister to have a relationship," Harmony says. "My mother too. It was good for me to forgive her."

"When are we going to get the dresses?" Kathy asked.

"I'm going to make sure that it's when the guys can go without you for a few hours. They will for me though," Harmony says. Beast comes over and pulls her away.

CHAPTER TEN: CRAZED

After we got back from the shopping Beast, and I put all the things in our rooms. "We are having a BBQ tonight. We deserve it with all the things we have been going through lately. Gorilla, Knuckles and Eagle go to the store. We need meat, sides, and drinks," Beast says.

"I want juice," Harmony says.

"We got you. What kind of juice you want?" Knuckles asked.

"Apple juice and Orange Juice," Harmony answers.

"Get some ribs and whatever else you decide you want. Make sure you grab some potato salad. We can set everything up while you are gone," Beast said.

"Okay," Gorilla says. They get in the SUV and go to the store.

"Let's get the grill set up and tables for the food," Beast orders and everyone gets to work. "You ladies sit down at the bar while we get everything together,"

"Yes Sir," Harmony says.

"I got your sir," Beast says. We got to work. Beast and I began pulling out tables. "What's going on between you two?"

"I'm in love with her and I don't want to fight it anymore," I answer.

"She deserves a great guy. I'm happy for you two," Beast says.

"I don't believe I deserve her love, but I plan to become someone that does," I reply.

"That's how I feel about Harmony," Beast says as he looks at her. "She is the best of me,"

"Josie and I are both broken but I want to be broken with her. She makes me want to be better," I say.

"Be right back," Beast says. I watch as he goes and gives Harmony a kiss. She says something and his face looks angry. I make eye contact with Josie. Chestnuts meet beautiful Emeralds. I smile at her. Beast comes back with an attitude.

"What happened?" I asked.

"They were talking about me," Beast answered.

"You do realize she knows how to get under your skin," I reply.

"I know," Beast replies.

"Then why do you let her," I asked.

"I don't know. She means the world to me," Beast answers.

"I can tell. Do you ever push her away," I asked.

"Not anymore. She stopped me from doing it. She showed me that I can be me without her judging me. She is a great woman," Beast answers.

"Does she talk to her mother any?" I asked.

"Yes. She is coming to the wedding with her husband and daughter. Harmony and her little sister talk every day. Her mother is moving up here to have a relationship with her. I think it will be good for her. She deserves the absolute best of everything," Beast says.

"She does. Where are you going for your honeymoon?" I asked.

"She doesn't want to go anywhere. She says she loves this place too much. Plus, you do know that the baby will be here any day now. She is having twins. So much has been going on lately that we don't have much fun. Tonight, is going to be good for us,"

Beast says. "Have you heard anything from the brother?"

"No. He disappeared before Josie went missing. I want to spend forever with her. I don't know if I should ask her," I answered.

"I think that would be good for both of you. Ask her at the reception. I think that would make Harmony happy. She really loves Josie," Beast answers.

"She has been getting in mama bear mode a lot lately," I replied as we finished setting up the table and chairs.

"I know. She is going to make a great mother. She is protective over the people she loves and cares about." I reply.

"The grills ready. All the table and chairs out here are put up. We are ready for the food," One of my brothers yelled from outside.

"Okay, Flight," Beast said. After we finished setting everything up, we waited for our brothers to come from the store so we could get everything ready. When they got back with the food, we set everything up. The food is cooking while the family and friends come. The party is going, and Harmony is sitting on Beast lap and Josie is sitting on mine. "Do you want something to drink?"

"I want some juice," Harmony answers. Beast waves his hand and tells one of the prospects to come closer.

"I'm good," Josie answered as we see one of the girls that hangs around walking up with another woman.

"Hello, Josie and Harmony, this is my sister Chantria. She just moved up here," the girl said.

"Hello, Lindsay. Hello Chantria," Harmony greets.

"It's nice to meet you," Chantria says as she waves at us.

"You can have a seat," Gorilla says. I look at Gorilla and he is watching her every move. She sits beside him. "I'm Gorilla,"

"It's nice to meet you," She answers.

"The pleasure is mine," Gorilla said. Her sister went off to do what she does best. She has a thing for Gunner, but he doesn't see her. There are only three girls left after Ashley stopped coming. Doll, Lolita, and Legs. The rest stopped coming after Beast got his old lady. They didn't know what happened to her. Harmony is protective over Beast. I'm glad that he found someone.

"How far along are you?" Chantria asked.

"They say between seven and eight months," Harmony answered.

"Are you having twins?" Chantria asked.

"They say only one, but I see twins. I'm big," She answered.

"You are sexy," Beast says as he rubs her belly. One of the prospects brings Harmony some juice.

"Thank you, Dewayne," Harmony says. He smiles then leaves to go look at the women.

"Why do you call everyone by their names?" Gorilla asked.

"It's a sign of respect Rashon," She answers.

"Okay," Gorilla replies. The music plays for a while, and we sit around. Everyone has eaten and the women with kids have already left. The rest of the party goes on before Beast and Harmony leave to go to bed.

"You ready," I asked, Josie.

"I thought you would never ask," Josie answered.

"You enjoy your time. I'm taking my woman to bed," I said. "Hold it down Gorilla," He nodded his head and went back to talking to the new girl. If it weren't for Doll, she never would have been there. Doll has been down and loyal to us since she started hanging here.

"Where is your mind at?" Josie asks.

"Here baby. Gorilla wants the nurse," I answered.

"She did seem cool. Gorilla is a great guy," Josie said as we got to our room. "I like when you take charge,"

"You do?" I asked.

"I love it," She answered.

"Good," I say as I close the door behind me. I gently lay her on the bed. I climb up her and start taking her clothes off. I'm kissing her as I'm taking her clothes off. When her clothes are on the floor, she starts taking mine off as she kisses me back. When we are both naked, she tells me to lay down. As soon as her mouth touched me, I became rock hard. She climbs on top of me and slides down. When I'm fulling inside of her, she began riding me. We make love for hours before we are completely sated. We lay on the bed wrapped together. He legs twist with mine as she lays on my chest. "I'm glad you chose me,"

"Me too," Josie answers. "You know I have never felt safe until you held me in your arms for the first time. I never want to lose that,"

"I don't ever want to lose you either. I love you," I say as I kiss her.

"I'm glad because you can't get rid of me even if you wanted too. If you ever leave me, I'm going with you. I love you," Josie says. I laugh and pull her closer to me if that is even possible. I watch her as she closes her eyes. I know she is asleep because her breathing softens. I close my eyes and follow her into the abyss.

CHAPTER ELEVEN: GORILLA

Beast and Crazed come into the building holding bags for their women. I'm happy for them. They leave out of the party hall. "We are having a BBQ tonight. We deserve it with all the things we have been going through lately. Gorilla, Knuckles and Eagle go to the store. We need meat, sides, and drinks," Beast says.

"I want juice," Harmony says.

"We got you. What kind of juice you want?" Knuckles asked.

"Apple juice and Orange Juice," Harmony answers.

"Get ribs and whatever else you decide you want. Make sure you grab potato salad. We can set everything up while you all are gone," Beast said.

"Okay," I answer. We get into the SUV and head to the store. We go into Kroger and begin shopping. We grabbed seven slabs of ribs, six packs of burgers, seven packs of hot dogs for the kids. As we are walking, I see the most beautiful woman I have ever seen. She has a young boy walking with her. I walk down the aisle I see her in.

"Mommie. Mommie, can I have spaghetti tonight?" The little boy yells.

"Okay," She answers. "I will make you some dinner before I go out with your auntie."

"Yay," The little boys say, jumping.

"Settle down," She orders. He listens. She gets the rest of her things and I watch her as she leaves.

"Damn did you have to follow her?" Knuckles asks. He has Harmony's juices in his hands.

"Did you see her?" I asked.

"Yeah. Not my type," Eagle said walking up with potato's salad.

"What other sides should we get?" Knuckles asked.

"Get baked beans, green beans, and potatoes. You know Mama will be mad if you don't get her the stuff to make homemade potato salad. Get mayo, pickled relish, sugar, mustard, and popsicles for the kids," I answered.

"You know he is right?" Knuckles said.

"I know," Eagle said. He left to get the things I said. We finished getting everything we could to make everyone happy. We got Pepsi, Coke, Sprite, Dr Pepper, water, juice, and juice cups. We headed back to our club. When we got back the guys took everything in the kitchen. Gunner got the meet ready and put them on the grill. Monsters wife was in the kitchen with the women cooking up the sides for tonight. After everything was ready, we started the party.

The party was going on for a while before all the mothers took their kids home for bed. Few of the men from town stayed for a while to party with us. We are sitting around laughing and talk when one of the girls that hang around came over with the woman, I saw at the store earlier. She was still looking as beautiful as she was at the store. I look around to see if I saw the little boy anywhere.

"Do you want something to drink?" Beast asks.

"I want some juice," Harmony answers. Beast waves his hand and tells one of the prospects to come closer.

"I'm good," Josie answered.

"Hello, Josie and Harmony, this is my sister Chantria. She just moved up here," The girl said.

"Hello, Lindsay. Hello Chantria," Harmony greets.

"It's nice to meet you," Chantria says as she waves at us.

"You can have a seat," I speak. I'm watching her every move. She sits beside me. "I'm Gorilla,"

"It's nice to meet you," She answers.

"The pleasure is mine," I reply. Her sister went off to do what she does best. She has a thing for Gunner, but he doesn't see her. There are only three girls left after Ashley stopped coming. Doll, Lolita, and Legs still come around, but the rest stopped coming after Beast got his old lady. We have a lot going on lately that the last thing we have time to think about is woman. We needed this party a lot. Beast got his woman and Crazed has his woman. I want to find one that I want to be with. I think I found her.

"How far along are you?" Chantria asked.

"They say between seven and eight months," Harmony answered.

"Are you having twins?" Chantria asked.

"They say only one, but I see twins. I'm big," She answered.

"You are sexy," Beast says as he rubs her belly. One of the prospects brings Harmony juice. Beast loves his woman.

"Thank you, Dewayne," Harmony says. He smiles then leaves to go look at the women.

"Why do you call everyone by their names?" I asked.

"It's a sign of respect Rashon," She answers.

"Okay," I reply. I don't mind her calling me by my name. She is the nicest person I have ever met. She has this light about her that shines bright. The music plays for a while, and we sit around. Everyone has eaten and the women with kids have already left. The rest of the party goes on before Beast and Harmony leave to go to bed.

"You ready," Crazed asked, Josie.

"I thought you would never ask," Josie answered.

"You enjoy your time. I'm taking my woman to bed," Crazed said. "Hold it down Gorilla," I nod my head and go back to the beautiful woman sitting beside me.

"How long are you here for?" I asked.

"Permanently," She answers.

"What brought you down here?" I asked.

"Ex that wouldn't let me be. I didn't want that kind of guy around my son," She answered. "Trey is his son, and he never came around unless he wanted something from me. He was sleeping with another woman and trying to control my every move. I didn't want my son growing up thinking it was okay for a man to just show up when it's convenient for him and not my son. My son deserves more," She answered. "He wanted me to be his old lady, but he didn't want to give up the whores or his wife."

"He is a biker?" I asked.

"Yes," She answered. "I was young and wild when I met him. My son is seven and I had him when I was nineteen. I'm twenty-six now,"

"I saw you with him earlier when I was at the store. He is a handsome young man," I said when she looks at me weird.

"Oh," she said.

"You are beautiful," I say looking into her beautiful eyes. I felt like I was staring at the ocean. "What is it that you do?"

"I'm a nurse at the local hospital," She answered.

"Nice," I replied.

"What do you do around here for fun?" She asked as her phone rang. She put her hand up and then walked off. I got up and followed behind her. "Hello," I watch her as she talks. "I really wish you would leave me alone. I'm not coming back. You didn't even want us. You are married and you tried to kill my son. I will never forgive you for that. You know that I was at work. You will never put your hands on me or my son again," She pauses. "I don't give a damn. I don't care what you want or what you keep saying you will do." I snatch the phone out of her hand. She looks at me like I lost my mind.

"She is with me now. She doesn't want to talk to you," I say, hanging up.

"Why did you do that?" She asked. "He is a dangerous man."

"I don't like seeing you stress and any man that tries to kill his own child doesn't deserve anything decent," I answer.

"You don't even know me," She countered.

"No, I don't but I want to. I want to know everything. No man should ever put their hands on a woman or a child. What happened exactly?" I asked.

"When I met him, he was so sweet. He brought me flowers. He took me on two dates. I was a virgin when we met. He talked me into having sex with him. He was such a sweet talker. He made me feel like I was the only woman in the world. We had sex and I got pregnant. I told him to put on a condom and he lied about putting it on. When I found out I was pregnant he told me to get rid of my child. I refused and it made him angry. He put me against the wall and choked me until I almost passed out. He had sex with me again whether I wanted it or not. Second time hurt just like the first. He left me alone for a while until he started coming around again apologizing for his behavior. I found out later that he was married," She answers then stops to take a deep breath. "Sorry. I don't know why I'm telling you any of this."

"I promise I won't tell anyone," I countered.

"Okay," She said. "I wasn't going to take him back, but he was persistent. I knew that he wasn't going to stop unless I did what he told me too. I found out he was sleeping with everyone when he brought me home an infection. Luckily for me it was a curable one. After that I told him to leave me alone. He wouldn't listen and kept coming around. When my sister asked me if I would move up here, I said yes. She never liked him. He just will not leave well enough alone,"

"Where did you move here from?" I asked.

"Wisher Wisconsin," She answers.

"That is kind of far, isn't it?" I asked.

"Far enough. I had to get as far away as possible from him. I don't want my son to see any man treating me like that," She replied.

"Yeah, we don't play games like that. You see the way my brothers treat their women. I have a little sister and I would kill someone if they ever did her the way he did you," I said.

"How old is your sister?" She asked.

"Twenty-seven," I answered.

"How old are you?" She asked.

"I'm thirty-one," I answered.

"Ewe you're an old man," She said, laughing.

"Funny," I replied, smiling.

"You have a nice smile," She said, blushing.

"You are just beautiful," I replied. She looked down trying to hide her face. I lifted her chin with my finger so she could look me in my eyes. "Never look down. You have nothing to hang your head for," Her phone began ringing again.

"It's my babysitter. Hold on," She said. "Hello," She gets silent for a minute. "Okay. I will be there soon. Tell him I'm coming," She hangs up. "My son woke up looking for me. It was great talking to you. I have to find my sister." I walked her into the building and helped her find Doll.

"You ready," Doll asked.

"Yes. Your nephew woke up looking for me," She answered.

"Hey, Gorilla can you take her home?" Doll asked. She was sitting on Gunner's lap. His army friend was sitting there talking to Lolita.

"I would love too," I say looking at her.

"That's fine," Chantria answered.

"I only have my bike where I can get it out," I said.

"I've never been on a bike," She said.

"Really," I asked.

"Yeah. He wouldn't let me go anywhere with him," She answered.

"Well let's go," I said as I took her hand. "Gunner keep everything under control. I will be back in minute," He nods and goes back to touching on Doll. We leave out of the building. I give her my helmet and she climbed on the back of my bike. When she wraps her arms around me, it feels like she is right where she needs to be. We get to where she is staying in ten minutes. I walk her to the door.

"Thank you. Hopefully, I will see you around," She said.

"If I have anything to do with it you will," I reply. I see her watching my lips as I talk. She smiles and I can't help myself. I wrap my hand around her neck and pull her to my lips. I kiss her like I have never kissed anyone ever before. Right when she started clinging to me, I pulled back. I put my forehead on hers, then backed away. "Have a great night," She walks in the house and closes the door behind her. Since I know she is safe I get on my bike and ride back to the club.

CHAPTER TWELVE: HARMONY

Today is the bridal shower and I'm excited. We got everything planned and set up for today. Tomorrow I'm marrying the only man I have ever loved. He is my entire world. I'm carrying his child and I can't wait to carry his last name. My best friend set everything up for the bridal shower. My mother and sister are here. They just moved last week down here in Kentucky. She wanted a relationship with me, and I wanted one with both, my sister, and my mother. "Harmony where are you at?" Josie asked.

"I'm back here. Did you finish setting up the games?" I asked coming out of the bathroom. We got a hotel and rented out the conference room for our little party.

"I did. Since tonight we are staying here so Beast doesn't see you, are we having a bachelorette party?" Josie asked.

"I'm too pregnant to party. I don't think the little one will let me be up to late." I answer. It's been three months since the incident with the man that hurt my friend and killed Brink. She has gotten better since her and Crazed finally stopped dancing around each other.

"Come back to me Harmony. Let's go," Josie said helping me walk out of the room. We go to the conference room where all the ladies and family are waiting.

"Harmony," My sister says running up to me. "I missed you," My mother nodded at me. When my sister was finished hugging me, my mother hugged me. We started the party. We played a few bridal shower games. After we finished with the games, we had cake and I opened presents. When we were finished, we went to the salon to get our hair and nails done. Josie had already got my dress and has my ring. After we finish with our hair and nails we go back to the room.

"Are you excited?" My sister asked.

"Very," I answer. "I love this man with everything that is in me. He may come across as rugged and rough, but he is gentle with me. He gave me meaning in my life. He gave me my child that I can't wait to hold for the first time."

"I'm happy for you. He does seem different with you than he is with anyone else. You are going to be a wife," My little sister said.

"Maybe we will have a second wedding soon," I countered looking at Josie.

"We are not there yet," Josie answered.

"You two look good together. You can tell you hang the moon with him. The way he looks at you is the way Beast looks at my sister," My sister says.

"I'm happy for you too," My mother says.

"Thanks mama. I'm glad you two could come. I wish my dad could have been here," I say looking at my fingers.

"He's here, Harmony," My mother said. I closed my eyes and could feel him close to me.

"Enough of the heavy. What do you want to do? I was going to take you to an all-male strip show but he would kill us. Plus, there wasn't one here," Josie said crunching up her face.

"It's all good. Jerome Jr will not let me get comfortable," I reply.

"I think there are two in there," Josie said.

"I do too. You are too big to just have one growing inside of you," My little sister joined in.

"I really don't care if there was three inside of me. I'm just excited to be a mother," I replied.

"I believe you will make a great mother," My mother said.

"I second that," Josie said, laughing.

"You sound like the guys," I pointed out.

"I know. That is why I laughed,"

"What next?" My sister asked.

"I'm ready to lay in the bed and watch a movie," I answer. "I'm wore out already,"

"Go get in bed I will bring us some fruit in," Josie said. I did what she told me to do? As soon as I laid in the bed my mother and sister climbed in with me. They left a space beside me for Josie. They know that Josie means the world to me, and she is my best friend. Josie climbs in beside me with a tray of fruit. I ate a few strawberries, watermelon, grapes, and bananas. My favorite fruit. I turn on a movie and start watching it. I don't know how long I watched before my eye lids started watching me.

******

Next thing I know I'm waking up in the morning getting ready to get married. I get out of the bed and Josie helps me get dressed for my wedding. I put my dress on and when I go outside there is a limo waiting on me. My family and I get in. When we get to the club house my family takes me through the back, so he doesn't see me. I'm finished and waiting for the wedding to start.

"I will be right back," Josie says as she goes to make sure everything is in its place. "Okay we are ready. Your stepfather will be here when it's your time to go," She kisses me on the cheek then leaves me to get in her spot. I'm getting anxious to get to my love. My stepfather takes my arm.

"Are you ready?" He asked. "You look beautiful. I'm honored that you allowed me to step in your fathers' place," He kissed me on the cheek.

"Thank you for accepting. I'm ready," I answer. As "She," is playing he walks me towards my man. He is smiling. He is the most handsome man in the world. All I see is him. I know that I will never want another man ever. He is my forever.

"Who gives this woman to this man?" The minister asked.

"I do," My stepfather says. He gives me to Jerome.

"Today we are gathered for the joining of these two hearts. In 1st Corinthians 13 verses 2-7 it says, If I have the gift of prophecy and can fathom all mysteries and all knowledge, and if I have a faith that can move mountains, but don't have love, I'm nothing. If I give all I possess to the poor and give over my body to hardship that I may boast, but don't have love, I gain nothing.

Love is patient, love is kind. It doesn't envy, it doesn't boast, it's not proud. It doesn't dishonor others, it's not self-seeking, it's not easily angered, it keeps no record of wrongs. Love doesn't delight in evil but rejoices with the truth. It always protects, always trusts, always hopes, always perseveres. The couple has vows that they would like to say," Minister says.

Beast says what he wants to say. I listen as my heart swells up. It's my turn to speak. "Growing up I didn't know what real love was supposed to look like. Then I met you. The love of my life, the man who makes my heart skip a beat when he looks at me. I love you and I promise to you on this day. I will forever be only yours. You brought light in my life when I thought it was always going to be dark. You showed me what real love looks like and showed me that I worth that love. Jerome, my handsome man, you are my everything and I plan to show you how much I absolutely love you for the rest of our lives," I say.

"Thank you. Jerome Grayson take out the ring," The minister says. Jerome listens to him. "With this ring I thee wed,"

"With this ring I thee wed," Jerome says. He puts the ring on my finger.

"Harmony Hall take out the ring," The minister says. I listen and do as I'm told. "With this ring I thee wed,"

"With this ring I thee wed," I say. I put the ring on his finger.

"Thank you. If any one doesn't believe these two should be married speak now or forever hold your peace," The minister says, pausing. "Since we have no objection. Mr. Jerome Grayson, you may now kiss your bride." Before I can say anything, Jerome pulls me to him and kisses me like the first time he ever kissed. We go sit in his favorite seat while everyone gets the reception ready.

"I have to get out of these clothes as soon as we take a picture," I say. Our photographer comes over in that moment.

"When the reception starts, I will began taking pictures. I will get one with the two of you. After I will get the entire wedding party," The lady says.

"Thank you,'" I reply. Everyone finishes getting everything ready and the caterer brings all the food. Everyone starts eating. When we finish eating, we take pictures. After taking the photos I get into something more comfortable. He had his leather on when we got married. I love it. He follows me into the room, and we make love for the first-time being husband and wife. After we head back to the party to have an exciting time dancing.

CHAPTER THIRTEEN: BEAST

Today is my bachelor party and my brother Crazed put it together. We go into the party hall which is set up for strippers. I could care less because they are not my woman. I love my woman and she is the most important in my world. I wonder want she is doing now. "Head in the game," Crazed said. He sat beside me.

"I'm not used to my woman not being here with me," I reply.

"I know. I got the ring. You want to see?" Crazed asked.

"Yeah," I answer. Crazed brings the ring out and shows it to me. It's a beautiful ring. "That's beautiful. She is going to love it."

"I hope so," Crazed answers. "Let's have some fun," The strippers come in and the guys love it. Crazed and I sat in the back and talked. Towards the end of the night a stripper danced on me. I wasn't interested but I let her do it. If Harmony saw it, she would have snatched her off me. That brought a smile to my face. My beautiful woman. We finished with the strippers. We sat around drinking and talking. When we finished talking, we went to bed. I was asleep within seconds.

******

The night passed and I woke up the next morning. It's my wedding day. I can't wait until I see her walking towards me. Her stepfather is walking her down the aisle. When I walked out into the party hall there was commotion everywhere. When everything is set up, I get into place. I wait as the music starts to play. Everyone in our wedding begins coming out. When they finished the song, I sang to her when I asked her to marry begins to play. I watch as the love of my life begins walking towards me. All I see is her. She smiles at me, and my heart skips a beat. "Who gives this woman to this man?" The minister asked when they get to me.

"I do," her stepfather says. The minister is talking but I don't hear anything. My focus is on her. Smells of vanilla and lavender hit my nose making me smile. Vanilla is her favorite smell. The minister gave me my cue.

"My life was at a standstill before I saw you. I knew at first glance that I had to have you. We have been through a lot, and I know we have a long life ahead of us. Eyes are like the ocean, and I become lost at sea when I look at you. Your smile brightens up my life. I believed I would spend the rest of my life missing something then you came. I will never be the same. I love you more than life itself. I will never leave you and I will protect you with my life. You are my sunshine, you are my breath, you are my hope, you are the woman that I will forever want and love. No one will ever come before you. You are my world. I love you," I say. She tells me her vows.

The minister finishes talking, and we put our rings on each other's finger. When he tells me to kiss my bride, I put my hand around her neck and pull her to me. I kiss her like I kissed her the very first time. My brothers get everything set up for the reception. We take pictures and dance. While eating we laugh and joke around. Crazed stands up. "I would like to make a toast," he says, tapping the glass. Everyone quiets down. "Me and my brother have been friends a long time. When he met Harmony, she was great for him. She showed us that she is strong and her love for her family is stronger. She is the loyal to only him. He couldn't have found a better match. Congratulations and I hope you have a long life together. You deserve it since you tamed the Beast," Everyone laughed.

Josie stood up. "Hello, it's my turn. I met Harmony when we were incredibly young. She was my hero. Few know she stopped two girls from bullying me when back then. When we finally talked, we became best friends. She was always my light in the darkness. She brings joy to everything that she touches. I'm glad she found someone that loves her as much as this man. I'm happy for you two. You deserve each other," Josie said, tears in eyes. We cut the cake and ate it. The party started. We danced for hours. Holding my wife in my arms felt right. I never want another in my arms.

"Cut the music," Crazed said. "Josie, can you come up here please?" Josie listens and makes her way to the front where he is. He takes her hand.

"He's about to do it isn't he?" Harmony asks.

"Yes. I saw the ring. It's beautiful," I answer.

"They deserve each other. They deserve happiness. We get to be in another wedding. I love you, Husband," She said.

"I love you more," He says. The song by Brian McKnight starts playing and Crazed sings,

"It's undeniable
That we should be together
It's unbelievable

How I used to say, that I'd fall never
The basis is needed to know
If you don't know just how I feel
Then let me show you now that I'm, for real
If all things in time, time will reveal
(Yeah, yeah)

One, you're like a dream come true
Two, just wanna be with you
Three, girl, It's plain to see
That you're the only one for me, and

Four, repeat steps one through three
Five, make you fall in love with me
If ever I believe my work is done
Then I'll start back at one
(Yeah, yeah)

It's so incredible
The way things work themselves out
And all emotional
Once you know what it's all about (hey)

And undesirable
For us to be apart
Never would've made it very far
'Cause you know, you've got the keys to my heart,
'cause

One, you're like a dream come true
Two, just wanna be with you
Three, girl, It's plain to see
That you're the only one for me, and

Four, repeat steps one through three
Five, make you fall in love with me
If ever I believe my work is done
Then I'll start back at one

Say farewell to the dark of night
I see the comin' of the sun
I feel like a little child, whose life has just begun
You came and breathed new life
Into this lonely heart of mine
You threw out the lifeline
Just in the nick of time

One, you're like a dream come true
Two, just wanna be with you
Three, girl, It's plain to see
That you're the only one for me, and

Four, repeat steps one through three
Five, make you fall in love with me
If ever I believe my work is done
Then I'll start back at one,"

When Crazed finishes singing, he got on one knee. She shakes her head yes. He picks her up and kisses her lips while everyone else claps.

CHAPTER FOURTEEN: JOSIE

The bachelorette party and wedding shower was fun. After the wedding we all sat around eating. It was beautiful watching my best friend and the love of her life get married. She deserves all the happiness in this world. I look over at my love and he is laughing with his brothers. They are a group of rugged men, but they are great men. They take care of their families. Crazed stands up to give a toast but I don't hear what he says because I'm amazed by his handsomeness. He is the most handsome man in the world. I understand why Harmony was the way she was with Beast.

I want to hold on to him and never let him go. I can still see the broken parts of him. I try my hardest to put those pieces back together. He smiles at me. It's my turn to speak. I stand up. "Hello, it's my turn. I met Harmony when we were incredibly young. She was my hero. Few know she stopped two girls from bullying me. When we finally talked, we became best friends. She was always my light in the darkness. She brought joy to everything that she touches. I'm glad she found someone that loves her as much as this man. I'm happy for you two. You deserve each other," I say. When I'm finished, I sit back down. We start dancing and having fun. We dance for hour and finally I sit down to rest my feet.

"Cut the music," Crazed said. "Josie, can you come up here please?" I look at him and I'm confused. I do what he asks and walk up to the front. The song back at one begins playing and Crazed starts singing. Tears are falling in waves down my cheek. He holds my hand as he sings to me. I didn't know he had such a sexy singing voice. He continues sings.

> One, you're like a dream come true
> Two, just wanna be with you
> Three, girl, It's plain to see
> That you're the only one for me, and

> Four, repeat steps one through three
> Five, make you fall in love with me
> If ever I believe my work is done
> Then I'll start back at one,"

He finishes and I watch him get on one knee. "Will you marry me?" I couldn't answer so I shook my head yes. I didn't want anything more than to be his wife. He stands up and I fall in his arms. He puts the ring on my finger. We dance for a few more hours before it happens.

"My water just broke," Harmony says as she sits in her seat. Beast runs to her and picks her up in his arms.

"Doc," Beast yelled.
"We have to get her to the hospital. Now Beast," Doc replied.
"Get the car," Beast orders.
"I'm on my way," Gorilla replied.

"My bag is in the room. Look in my closet," Harmony says. I run to the room and grab her bag. I know she will need this stuff after the baby is born. We pile into the SUV. Crazed and I climbed into the back seat. Gorilla was driving.

"Harmony baby I need you too breath," Beast said softly. We get the hospital and park. Beast carry's Harmony inside the building. "She's in labor. Can we get some help?"

"Jerome baby you can put me down," Harmony says.

"Beast here. I brought these in," I say.

"Thanks Josie," Beast says.

"Harmony I'm coming too," I say.

"Hell, yes you are," Harmony says.

"Deiondre, you have to stay out here baby," I say as we go back to the emergency room. We get to the room and the Ob-gyn comes in to check on her. After he figures out how far along, she is they take her to the fourth floor to the baby wing. Harmony is breathing erratically, and they are trying to stop her pain. She is seven centimeters dilated when the doctor checks.

"Another one is coming," Harmony screams.

"Breath baby," Beast says as he breaths with her. This happens for a while before she cries out.

"I feel like I have to push," She says. "Get the doctor," I call for the doctor he comes in and checks her.

"The baby is coming," The doctor says getting her legs ready. "Push," Harmony begins pushing. She keeps pushing. "Breath," She listens. "Push," She begins pushing again. "I see the head. Keep pushing," She pushes, and the baby comes out. The doctor cuts the umbilical cord.

"Why am I still having contractions and feel like I have to push again?" Harmony asks.

"Push. I see another head," The doctor says sitting back down. Harmony listens, and the second baby comes out. "First is a boy and the second is a girl," He cuts the umbilical cord, and the nurses sit both babies on her chest. I smile at them.

"I'm going to tell the guys and give you too a minute," I say as Beast sits on the bed beside harmony and holds her.

"These are our babies," Beast says as I softly closed the door. I go down to the first floor so everyone can come to the right floor. When I get down everyone was in the waiting room except Gorilla.

"She had the babies," I say.

"Babies," Tank asked.

"Two. One boy and one girl," I answer. Monster gets up and goes outside. "I left them in the room to spend some time with their babies. We have to go up to the fourth floor." We wait for Gorilla to come back in the building. When he comes in a beautiful woman is coming in right before. "Who was that?"

"G got a thing for the nurse," Tank says.

"Shut it," Gorilla says. "What's up?"

"We got twins," I answer.

"Twins?" Gorilla asks.

"Yes. One boy and One girl," I answer. "Follow me." I head to the fourth floor. When we get there, we have a seat in the waiting room. "I'm going to see what is going on," I go back to the room she was in.

"I have to stay a couple of nights. Isn't it amazing our children's birthday is on our wedding anniversary. I love it," Harmony says, smiling.

"Have you decided what the names are going to be?" I asked.

"Jerome Grayson Jr and Patience Grayson. I'm exhausted. They are going to take me to a room in a few," Harmony says closing her eyes.

"You know she gets what she wants. I think they gave her morphine. She is asleep. Let's go out and let her sleep for a little while," Beast says. He kisses her on her forehead. "I'm going to talk to the guy's baby. I will be back," When she didn't respond we left out of the room. "When you move her will you get me. I'm going to step out and talk to my family,"

"Yes sir," The young nurse says looking him up and down.

"Really. He just had babies with his wife. Stop it," I say shaking my head. The young girl's eyes widened. She was caught checking him out. Beast didn't seem to notice. That is when I knew he only had eyes for Harmony. "You really didn't notice her checking you out?"

"No. The only woman that I care about is the one in there sleeping. No one has anything on her," Beast answers as we head into the waiting room.

"Congrats on the new babies. We have two to spoil now," Tank said.

"Man, you are one lucky guy," Monster said holding his wife in his arms.

"Babies are a blessing. Cherish them because they grow up fast," Monster's wife says. "Congrats son."

"Thank you," Beast replies.

"How does it feel?" Gorilla asks.

"It feels great. I created two lives, and I will cherish them for the rest of my life. Harmony is going to make a great mother," Beast says, smiling.

"Brink would have been proud," Toast says.

"Yes, he would have," Beast says.

"How long are they going to keep them?" Doc asked.

"Three days. They will make sure they are healthy and good to go. Let's see if we can see them in the nursery," Beast says. When we get to the nursery, we can tell which are his. They look just like him.

"They are beautiful," Eagle says.

"Yes, they are," Beast says, smiling. They get Harmony into her room and take care of her. I stay at the hospital as much as I can. Beast barely leaves her side. He will leave when there is a meeting or figure something out at the club. When he leaves, I stay with her. We get her and the babies ready to take home. While she has been in the hospital, I got the nursery ready. The babies will be in the room with her. We get the babies in their car seats, and she gets checked out. Crazed drove the SUV here. We put the babies in the truck and head home.

When we get to the house everyone is waiting for her to come. They set up banners and everything for the babies. When we get in the building everyone yells surprise and we party until it's time to feed the babies and put them to bed. I helped her feed and get the babies ready. I help her pump milk out for the babies. After she has a lot pumped and, in their bottles, we feed them. She takes her baby boy and I take the baby girl. After we feed them, we rock them to sleep and put them in bed. We tippy toe out of the room and close the door softly. The party is still going. We head back out to where the guys are.

Harmony sits on Beasts lap for a little while before they retire to the bedroom. I sit on Crazed lap and smile at him. "How are the babies?" He asked.

"They are fast asleep. They are precious. I want one," I say.

"Well let's go make one then," Crazed said as he kissed me on my lips.

"What are we waiting for?" I asked. He picks me up and carries me to our bed. That night he made love to me all through the night.

CHAPTER FIFTEEN: CRAZED

The bachelor party went by without a problem. I'm so happy for my brother and his woman. My brother deserves to be happy. We have been through a lot. He has been my brother since we were in diapers. He has always had my back and I will always have his. Losing Brink took a toll on all of us. It's harder for Toast, Beast, and me because he died protecting our women and Toast was his best friend. Brink was a great guy. The wedding is in full effect now and we are dancing the night away. Well, it seems like it's night, but it's not. We are just having fun. I watch as Josie dances with Harmony. She is beautiful. She looks at me and my heart flutters. She is my world and I want to spend the rest of my life with her.

She is using her finger telling me to come to her. I do as I'm told. When I get to her, I rap my arms around her hips. I pull her to me. "I love you,"' I say.

"I love you too," Josie replies. A slow song comes on and we dance to the beat. Her body is close to mine. Vanilla hits my nose as I twirl her around. She giggles and I know she likes it. She needs to feel like a princess because after tonight if she has me, I will make her my queen. She goes and takes a seat. It's time. I head to the stage. "Cut the music," I say. "Play "Back at one," by Brian McKnight after she gets up here," He nods at me. "Josie, can you come up here please?" She looks at me confused. She listens and comes to me. I take her hand and the DJ plays the song. As I'm singing her the words she begins to cry.

One, you're like a dream come true
Two, just wanna be with you

Three, girl, It's plain to see
That you're the only one for me, and

Four, repeat steps one through three
Five, make you fall in love with me
If ever I believe my work is done
Then I'll start back at one,"

I get down on one knee. "Will you marry me?" I ask. She nods her head. I get back up and she falls into my arms where she belongs. I put the ring on her finger. We dance for a few more hours until Harmony yells from her seat.

"My water just broke," Harmony says. Beast runs to her and picks her up in his arms.

"Doc," Beast yelled.

"We have to get her to the hospital. Now Beast," Doc replied.

"Get the car," Beast orders.

"I'm on my way," Gorilla replied.

"My bag is in the room. Look in my closet," Harmony says. Josie leaves and comes back with a bag in her hand. We pile into the SUV. Josie is in the back with me. Gorilla drives us to the hospital.

"Harmony baby I need you too breath," Beast said softly. We get the hospital and park. Beast carry's Harmony inside the building. "She's in labor. Can we get some help?"

"Jerome baby you can put me down," Harmony says.

"Beast here. I brought these in," Josie says.

"Thanks Josie," Beast says.

"Harmony I'm coming too," Josie says.

"Hell, yes you are," Harmony says.

"Deiondre, you have to stay out here baby," Josie says. She is the only person that can call me that besides Harmony. That is just what she does. They take Harmony to the back, and I sit in the waiting room seat.

"Where is Josie?" Gorilla asks.

"She went back with Beast and Harmony," I answer. Everyone else sits down and starts talking very loudly.

"For real I was about to get in some pussy. She was sucking me up before we heard," Tank says.

"I was about to have some fun with Doll," Gunner said.

"You do know that she only messes with you right?" Gorilla said.

"Excuse me can you guy keep it down please. This is a hospital," The nurse that took my family back says. I think she was at the party. Dolls sister.

"You heard her," Gorilla said.

"Oh shit, Gorilla is sweet on her. Isn't she the girl from the BBQ three months ago?" Tank asks.

"Shut it, Tank," Gorilla grates. I laugh to myself. I know what it felt like when it happened to me.

"What? I was just saying what I see," Tank says, Laughing.

" Yeah. G got a crush," Gunner says.

"Shit it, Gunner," Gorilla retorts. My brothers start laughing. The nurse leaves the building and so does Gorilla.

"You do know that one day you are going to find your woman and they will do you the same way," I say. "She just shows up out of nowhere."

"Sprung," Crow said.

"Ha, Ha, Ha," I say. "I'm telling you. I can be sprung. At least I have someone that loves me for me and not what I can give her." I don't say anything else. A little while later Josie comes out and tells us they had twins. We go to the fourth floor to wait until Beast comes out to talk to us. We talk for a while then see the babies. They are the most beautiful things I have ever seen. We get to give them the lives we never got as kids. Our biker lifestyle is great but with kids around we have to stop a lot of the sex in the open they used to do.

We are going to be all right. "You can go home. I'm staying. Josie is going with you all," Beast says. I nod. Beast goes to the back and Josie comes out. We head home for the night. We go to bed and end it with making love. We fell asleep wrapped in each other's arms. When we woke up in the morning we were refreshed.

******

Three days later Harmony and the babies come home. We have everything set up to welcome them home. We got two new editions to our family. We all yell surprise and go to partying. Harmony hangs with us for while then leaves with Josie to put the babies to bed. Josie had been staying at the hospital when Beast had to leave. Josie set up the nursery and made sure the cribs were put up. She will make an amazing mother one day. We will protect our babies better than our parents protected us. "How's it feel being a father," I ask.

"It's the greatest feeling in the world. Harmony has changed since she had the babies. She is more protective if that is possible. She keeps getting in Mama bear mode. She scares me," Beast answers.

"I'll show you scared," Harmony says. Her and Josie walk up. She sits on Beast lap. He holds her. They sit out here with us for a while before they retire to the bedroom.

"How are the babies?" I asked.

"They are fast asleep. They are precious. I want one," Josie says.

"Well let's go make one then," I say as I kiss her on my lips.

"What are we waiting for?" I asked. I pick her up and carry her to our bed. That night I made love to her all through the night. Not stopping until the sun came up the next morning.

EPILOGUE

Gorilla

"My water just broke," My brother's wife said, yelling from her seat. One minute we were dancing and having fun at the reception. The next minute Harmony's water broke.

"Doc," My brother yelled.

"We have to get her to the hospital. Now Beast," Doc replied.

"Get the car," Beast orders.

"I'm on my way," I replied. I grabbed the SUV and pulled it around. We got her into the SUV. Crazed and Josie climbed into the very back.

"Harmony baby I need you too breath," Beast said softly. She listened to him, and I drove her to the hospital. We get her to the hospital and Beast carries her inside. I park the truck and head into the building. Harmony and Beast were nowhere to be found. I heard the bikes in the distance. Our family is coming. With everything that has been going on lately, it's great to have something beautiful coming into the world. The rest of our family pulls into the hospital parking lot. After they park, we head inside. We find Crazed sitting in the waiting room.

"Where is Josie?" I ask.

"She went back with Beast and Harmony," Crazed answers. We all sit down but began talking loudly.

"Excuse me can you guy keep it down please. This is a hospital," The sweetest voice I have ever heard said. I look up to see a scowl on her face. She looks at me and I see the most beautiful emeralds I have ever seen. I don't look at her for too long before she turns on her heels and leaves us there.

"You heard her," I said when they started talking again.

"Oh shit, Gorilla is sweet on her. Isn't she the girl from the BBQ three months ago?" One of my brothers said.

"Shut it Tank," I grated.

"See what I mean," Tank says.

"Yeah. G got a crush," Another brother said.

"Shut it, Gunner," I grated. They all started laughing.

******

Chantria

"She's in labor," I heard someone say as he carried a beautiful chestnut colored hair woman in. "Can we get some help?"

"Jerome baby you can put me down," The woman said.

"Beast here. I brought these in," Another woman said handing him a bag.

"Thanks Josie," Beast said.

"Harmony I'm coming too," Josie said.

"Hell, yes you are," Harmony replied.

"Deiondre, you have to stay out here baby," Josie said as we guided them to the emergency room. I went to a party with my sister, they were there. I can hear the bikes in the distance. I loved one before, he got me pregnant. He tried to beat the child out of me, but he didn't succeed. I barely made it out alive. I never even tried to find him after that. He found me, but I wasn't falling for his lies again. He started stocking me even though he had a wife and whores he slept with every night. That is why I moved five hundred miles away. Not long after about fifteen bikers came into the lobby. I'm hoping I see the one that kissed me. I haven't been able to get him out of mind since I felt his lips on mine.

"For real I was about to get in some pussy. She was sucking me up before we heard," One of the bikers said loud.

"I was about to have some fun with Doll," Another said. That's my sister.

"Excuse me can you guy keep it down please. This is a hospital," I grated. The guy who kissed me, looked up and we made eye contact. His eyes a beautiful chestnut that match his mocha skin. I like cocoa. He was beyond handsome. I turned away and headed back behind the counter.

"You heard her," I heard the sexy man say.

"Oh shit, Gorilla is sweet on her. Isn't she the girl from the BBQ three months ago," One of the bikers said.

"Shut it Tank," Gorilla grated.

"What? I was just saying what I see," Tank says.

"Yeah. G got a crush," Another biker said.

"Shut it, Gunner," Gorilla grated. They all started laughing. I didn't find it that funny. Just then my phone rings. I look at the number but don't know it. I know it's not the babysitter because I have her number saved in my phone. I go grab one of my coworkers to take my spot. I'm a nurse but we are so shorthanded that I was checking people in. I head outside to call the number back. Before I can dial the number my phone rings again.

"Hello," I answer.

"Hey baby," The one voice I never wanted to hear again says.

"Don't hey baby me. I told you to leave me alone. How did you get this number?" I grated.

"You can't go too far without me finding you," He said. "You belong to me,"

"I belong to no one. You need to leave me alone. I moved away to get away from you," I answered.

"I don't care," He countered.

"Where is your wife?" I asked.

"Does it matter? I own both of you," He grated.

"You don't own me. Leave me alone. Just because you lied and got me pregnant doesn't mean you own me. You tried to kill me and your son when you found out I wouldn't kill him in my belly. It was by God that you didn't. If you contact me again, I will get a restraining order on you," I countered.

"If you do that, I will kill you and your son," He grated.

"Don't threaten me or my son," I answered as my phone was taken out of my hand. I turned and Cocoa has my phone to his ear.

"If you want to get to her or her child you have to go through me. If you were any type of man, you would never threaten to harm to any woman or child," He said then hung up the phone.

"Who do you think you are? Just because you kissed me once doesn't give you the right," I grated.

"I heard the whole conversation. I didn't like him talking to you like that," He countered.

"You don't know me," I countered.

"I don't have to know you to want to protect you. No man should every threaten to touch or harm a woman or child. Especially if that child is his," He answered.

"I moved her to get away from him. I changed my number and everything. He still found me," I said as I looked down at the ground.

"Don't ever hang your head," He said as he took his finger and lifted my chin.

"The baby is here Gorilla," One of the bikers said peeking out of the door.

"Thanks Monster," Gorilla said.

"I have to get back to work. Thank you. He isn't going to let me go that easy though," I said and began to go back into the building.

"If he knows what is good for him then he will," Gorilla said stopping me in my tracks.

"What does that mean?" I asked.

"He will find out if he tries anything. Just know that you are protected," Gorilla said.

"I don't need anyone to protect me. I can take care of myself," I grated. I didn't like him thinking that he needed to protect me.

"That isn't what I'm saying," Gorilla replied, calmly.

"Then what are you saying?" I asked.

"I want to protect you," Gorilla said.

"Why?" I asked.

"Since I kissed your lips, I can't get you out of my head," Gorilla said. I could relate but I wasn't going to tell him that. I could feel my cheeks heating up. Before I knew what was happening, he had me pinned to the wall. His lips connected with mine and I lost it. I kissed him back. I don't know how long I kissed him before he pulled away. He walked away from me. I got myself together before I headed back into the hospital.

******

Gorilla

It's been three weeks since the babies were born. Most of Beast time has been towards his new babies. Harmony is even more protective than Beast. She takes care of us guys. She makes sure we eat every night. Beast is lucky to have such a great woman. Between her and Josie us guys are taken care of to the fullest. I can't seem to get the woman out of my head. Chantria's eyes haunt me in my dream. I dream about laying her down and owning her. She doesn't know it yet, but she will be mine.

"G. Your girl is here," Toast says coming into the kitchen. Our brother we lost in keeping Josie safe is still missed. I head to the front of the building. When I get there Chantria is standing there with tears in her eyes.

"What's wrong?" I ask.

"Someone has been stalking me," She says.

"Do you know who it is?" I ask.

"It's him. It a recording and I don't know whose voice it is. They keep telling me that they are going to take my son if I don't stop talking to you," She says.

"Why don't you and your son come stay here with me until I get to the bottom of it," I say.

"Are you sure that is what you want?" She asked. "You don't owe me anything,"

"Go pack your things and I will talk to my brothers. Make sure that you lock your doors until I come with the SUV and get you," I say. She nods. I pull her to me and kiss her lips. She doesn't stop me. I watch as she gets in her little car and leaves the compound. I go to find Beast.

"What's up?" Beast asks as I walk back into the kitchen.

"You okay," Harmony asks.

"You remember the nurse from the hospital?" I ask.

"Yes. She was a pretty thing," Harmony says. "What's wrong?"

"She is getting harassed by someone. They are telling her if she doesn't leave me alone, they will hurt her and her son," I answer.

"Is she yours?" Beast asked.

"Yes. She may not know it yet but yes," I answer.

"We will have a meeting and talk to the guys," Beast says. I go into the meeting room. "Meeting. Everyone in. That includes the prospects," Usually, we don't include the prospects, but it's close to them becoming brothers. We will vote next month. Everyone piles in. "I called this meeting because our brother needs our help,"

"Everyone remember the nurse?" I asked. Everyone nodded. "She just came by. Someone is calling her telling her they are going to hurt her and her son if she doesn't stay away from me. I'm thinking it's Ashley's brother. We haven't heard from him in a while. It may be her kid's dad. He tried to kill her son when he was in her stomach and after he was born," I say. "I want her to come here so I can keep her safe,"

"I have one question," Crazed asked. "Is she yours?"

"Yes," I answer.

"Then she will always be protected," Crazed replied.

"I'm with that," Tank said.

"Everyone okay with another protection put your hand in the air," Beast said. Everyone raised their hand. "That's it. Get your woman. Eagle, Toast, and Tank go help him out. Get what she needs and if she ends up staying with you, we can move the rest then. Help her get everything she needs. Her and the boy can have one of the empty rooms," I nod then leave to get my woman.

ABOUT THE AUTHOR

I'm a thirty-eight-year-old wife, mother, co-worker, daughter, student, and author. I have been writing for years now. This is my seventh book I have finished since my first one ten years ago. I'm currently going back to school to get my bachelor's degree in Creative writing. I love to spend time with my husband who is the love of my life. My son just turned eighteen in July, and it feels weird to have a grown child. I have quite a few people that support me and believe in me. I don't have to say names for you to know those to whom I'm talking. Thank you for all your support.
 Below are books in order of publication.

All Books can be found on amazon or you can contact me by email.

When Life Makes You Cry
A Love So Strong.
Blind Color: Blinded By Blood
The Dragon's Hunt.
Learning How To Love
Beauty's Beast- The Black Angels Mc Book 1-If you have not read it first then you might want to because you meet the characters that are in book 2.
Contact Information-
Facebook-Talitha Gholston
tntwritingandmore.weebly.com
authortalithag@gmail.com/mrsgholston30@gmail.com

Taming Gorilla is in the works. Book 3 of The Black Angels MC

Made in the USA
Columbia, SC
27 January 2024

30346830R00069